An abandoned home on a north woods lake,
dreams of a seductive lover from another time.
Lindsay wants the hundred-year-old home to heal her troubled
marriage,
something unseen in the house wants her.

"I loved this story and was immediately drawn into the storyline,
wanted to know what was happening to Lindsay. There were
plenty of twists to keep me turning the pages to see what was
going to happen next."
TOP PICK!
Night Owl Reviews

"Supernatural stories require readers to suspend disbelief, and
Hill accomplishes that difficult feat. She seductively pulls the
reader into this haunting story as only a skilled writer can do."
Elizabeth Grandy,
Desert Soliloquy

"One of the best books I've read in a long time."
E Persons

"A totally different ghost story that captivated me and kept me
up well beyond my normal bedtime."
L. Powell

**READERS ADVISORY: Contains love scenes
with graphic language**

L. Cooper Press

LCP

Cover by Coverfresh Designs
Formatting by Polgarus Studio

Author's Note:

While I'm currently a California-based author, I lived for several years next to Serpent Lake in Crosby, a picturesque town of less than three-thousand in north/central Minnesota.

During the long, snowbound winters, I would walk my dog past homes owned by snowbirds, those owners who spent the harsh winters in warmer climates, and imagine stories that might take place in those houses sitting cold and abandoned during the sub-zero winters.

I always strolled through the lakeside park to gaze in wonder at Kahnah'bek, the twenty-foot-high fiberglass serpent statue reigning supreme over the grounds. There, during the quiet that blanketed the land immediately after a snowfall, I'd let my imagination soar. The House on Serpent Lake is the result.

ACKNOWLEDGMENTS

Mike Midthun, Dispatch/Records Mgr/Evidence Tech, Crosby, MN Police Department and super nice guy. Thanks for taking the time to answer questions and to photograph various sites for me. Although I lived next to Serpent Lake for a number of years, the pictures helped to refresh my memory.

Kd Foreman, Director, Lead Investigator - Cal~Para Paranormal Research Organization. Thanks for tolerating the endless questions on a fascinating subject and for allowing me to see and handle some of the equipment you use during an investigation. I hope I got it all right.

Joanna Lattery, Mayor of Crosby, MN, my thanks for being so gracious. Charles Barnum III, Attorney at Law, Jason Evans, attorney at Law, Paula Traylor and Jessica Holmvig with the Crosby Chamber of Commerce.

Mae Phillips of Coverfresh Designs for the cover and Jason Anderson for formatting.

Fellow authors Victoria Howard, M. Jean Pike, Libby Grandy, Millie Hinkle, and Merri Hiatt. To friends Maxine Piotrowski, Elizabeth Walker Persons, Linda Powell, Brandon G. Cole, D.C., Mary Bowman, Bob and Sheila Dearmore, Janice McFarland. Thanks y'all, for your encouragement and support.

And always, my love and thanks to Roger Bowman, who dropped everything countless times to respond to my SOS calls. To Amanda and Kyle, the lights in my life.

The Intruder

The Past
Crosby, MN

A brief hushed whisper floated up the stairs and disturbed the young woman's dreams.

Frida Peterson woke.

Listening intently, she lay in the feathered bed and wondered what she'd heard. From the window, the normal night sounds from the north woods behind the house were in full concert—chirping crickets, buzzing katydids, and from the marshy area skirting Serpent Lake in front of the house, frogs bellowed, the cacophony of their sawing, hiccupping noise almost drowning out the other sounds.

But nothing out of the ordinary.

She listened a few more minutes, then closed her eyes and tried to go back to sleep.

Then she heard it again. A woman's soft moan, a sound so out of the ordinary that she caught her breath. She sat up.

Frida pointed the gun and fired three rounds into the man's back.

Everything froze. Even the night creatures went silent.

Berina screamed.

The man stiffened, turned and faced her, his face frozen in shock. Like a fan folding in on itself, he slowly crumpled to the floor. Berina, her face and gown splattered with blood, screamed and fell beside him, gently cradling the man's head in her arms.

Tilly rushed into the room, tying her chenille robe. "Oh, missy, what have you done?"

Soundlessly, her eyes wide, Frida stared at the bloodied man's face. The gun fell from her hand and hit the oak floor.

A sound, a wailing, keening cry of agony filled the room. She didn't know if it came from Berina or from her.

Galen, the man she loved with all her heart, the man she was to marry in three weeks, was dead.

Chapter One

The Present
Crosby, MN

Something about the abandoned old house struck Lindsay Peterson as familiar.

It sat about a quarter-mile past the modern homes lining Serpent Lake, off a deeply-rutted trail skirting the aspens and pines of the Minnesota north woods.

They drove closer, Lindsay shading her eyes against the setting sun's glare on the lake. Beyond low-hanging branches, she could see the two-story house and several outbuildings in a clearing by the water.

"We're here." Eric guided the rented Blazer along the ruts to a detached garage. "I know it's been a long day, but let's take a quick look before it gets dark." He killed the engine and lowered the windows.

Mosquitoes invaded the car and whined around Lindsay's head. When one lit on her arm, she slapped it and wiped the blood speck with a tissue.

Eric bounded out of the car as if his aunts were still waiting to welcome him, but Lindsay sat frozen, her gaze moving over the house, lingering at the large side window. She knew that house, knew how the rooms were arranged, knew how it felt to wake each morning with her window overlooking the woods in the back of the house. She caught phantom aromas of fresh biscuits from the oven, the huge lilac bushes around the outhouse coupled with the earthy scent of the water.

She nearly wept with longing.

"Come on," Eric said, waiting for her in front of the car. "Aren't you curious?"

At the sound of his voice, the déjà vu dissipated, floating away as if it were a dream she couldn't quite remember.

Frowning, she looked back at the house, which was now simply neglected property her husband had inherited. This was her first trip to Minnesota, so she couldn't know anything about the house and grounds. She must have seen pictures or Eric must have described his childhood home so thoroughly she felt she knew every detail.

That's all it was, wasn't it?

Firmly pushing away her doubts, she emerged from the car. After the long flight from the west coast, followed by another three-hour shuttle from the Minneapolis airport, all she wanted was a hot meal and a comfortable bed at the motel. But Eric was his aunt's only surviving relative and Lindsay wanted to support her husband even if it meant touring the dilapidated property at dusk.

She stepped onto an overgrown lawn littered with twigs and bits of pinecones and followed her husband through thick patches of dandelions gone to seed. Wisps of soft white fuzz floated in the air.

The house hadn't fared any better. Curls of white paint hung over blackened windows, and bare rotting wood spread under chipped paint.

"I don't understand it," Eric said, forging ahead, his long legs cutting through tall grass to the front of the property. "It's such a nice place, at least it used to be. I wonder what happened?"

Following him, Lindsay couldn't venture a guess, especially when she spotted the fully-screened front porch facing the water. True, it might be sagging, but it fronted two-hundred feet of sandy beach and the tree-lined lake. How ideal it all seemed, even with the house in its current state of disrepair.

"Maybe your aunt failed to make arrangements for caretakers after moving to the nursing home," she said.

"Aunt Frida wouldn't forget. Grandpa built this place, even cleared the land himself, and she'd never let it deteriorate. Besides, her attorney was supposed to take care of all that." Hands on his hips, he considered the house. "I just hope the inside is okay. All hardwood floors and a huge rock fireplace. You'll love it. Aunt Frida used to tell stories about Grandpa searching the countryside for just the right stones."

"It doesn't look vandalized," Lindsay said. "Just neglected. But we'll find out when we pick up the keys in the morning."

Eric headed toward a faded log building about twenty feet from the house. A rusty shovel leaned against the side, its splintered wooden handle enclosed in cobwebs.

"The old storage shed." He jiggled the lock. When it fell open, he disappeared inside. Lindsay smiled, her pride in her husband overriding her fatigue.

He was such a nice-looking man, one of the lucky ones who improved with age. At forty-seven and even with a little thickening at the waist, his bearing was proud and strong.

And he was tall enough so she didn't tower over him, something she'd agonized over since her teenage years. Once again, she thanked the fates for bringing them together two years ago. After a failed three-year marriage in her early youth, she hadn't bothered with much of anything except raising her son—until she met Eric and the world came alive.

She lifted her face to the gentle breeze that whispered across the lake, stirring leaves in the oak trees and gently ruffling her hair.

Suddenly, as though eyes were watching her, little prickles chilled the back of her neck. Whirling around, she stared at the darkened windows in the house, but she saw nothing except the black panes standing as sentries, guarding the house's secrets.

Eric emerged from the shed and closed the squeaky door and joined her on the beach.

She glanced back at the house and it seemed normal. Old, in need of repair, but normal.

Eric brushed cobwebs from his shoulders. "Pretty well cleaned out except for some old tools. Strange, though. Someone's half-eaten lunch and an old rusted thermos were splattered on the floor. Someone left in a hurry."

Another mosquito lit on her forearm. "Mosquitoes probably got them," she said, slapping it, wishing she'd worn her jacket on the trip instead of the short-sleeved linen pantsuit.

"Don't you like it?"

"Mosquitoes the size of pigeons and a decaying old house. What's not to like?"

"Oh." His disappointment was evident and Lindsay's heart melted.

"I was teasing, honey. Of course I like it. You know I've always wanted to live next to the water. It'll make a great vacation home and I can't wait." She leaned forward to give him a kiss, but before she could touch him, a sudden gust of wind blew off the lake, swirling sand and leaves in the air. Bits of grit peppered Eric's face. The wind rushed over the grounds, moaning as it whooshed through the house.

Just as suddenly, it died.

"What was that?" Lindsay asked, staring at the house.

Eric rubbed his eyes. "Lots of breezes from the lake. Cools things down in summer."

"That wasn't a breeze, that was a gale. You okay?" She brushed his lips with hers, but instead of returning the kiss, he broke contact and backed away.

"I'll check the house," he mumbled, avoiding her eyes. "It's probably locked, but I'll give it a try. Then we can go." He cut away from her and raced across the lawn. She wished she could laugh at his hasty retreat. Instead, she nearly cried.

Was he more upset about losing his aunt than she'd thought? After all, Frida was the last living link to his family. But no, she had noticed his withdrawal months earlier.

Even though she didn't want to admit it, something was wrong in their marriage.

As a computer consultant to large corporations all over Southern California, he traveled two to three days a week, and his homecoming was cause for celebration. During the first few months of their marriage, she'd take time off from the art gallery she owned and they'd loved and played like newlyweds.

But that had gradually changed.

She couldn't say exactly when it had happened, but he began volunteering for every trip that came up. And when he was home, he acted strangely … distant. He'd avoid coming to bed until she was asleep.

Was it something she'd done, or did he no longer find her attractive? He had assured her nothing was wrong, that he'd just been working too many hours. They needed the extra income, he'd said, for a down payment on a house large enough for both their children to visit. Their condo was only a one bedroom, so it sounded reasonable. But the distance between them had not improved.

Shrieking gulls caught her attention. She watched them circle over the water and dive for a meal.

The sun dipped behind the tree-lined west shore, and in the growing dusk, the sky burned a fiery red. Clouds picked up the glow, painting long crimson streaks as far as she could see. Below, their mirror images danced on the gentle swells of the water. Lindsay didn't know if she'd ever seen anything so beautiful.

What a haven this could be, miles from the pressures of Eric's work. They could rediscover each other and put the fire back into their marriage.

Lindsay pictured the house freshly painted and the grounds trimmed and neat. Finally, a true home of her own, something she had always wanted but never thought she'd have.

Growing up with a single mother who moved every couple of years, never knowing a home or family except for distant grandparents, her life had always seemed empty. When her first husband came along and professed to love her, she'd hastily married. Then, except for her son, emptiness again. And now this house and grounds. Even neglected it represented love and strong family roots.

They'd paint it white, like it used to be, with black trim around the windows, and … used to be? Where had that thought come from?

She must have seen photos.

A swing would be perfect, exactly right for those quiet evenings at home. She was scanning the porch for the perfect spot when suddenly, a curious sadness began, spreading into a grief so strong and heavy that her knees almost buckled under the weight. Tears spilled onto her cheeks.

Bewildered, she brushed them away and stared at the house. What would cause her to feel such sorrow? Was it because it had been a home for a family, and she was afraid she was losing hers?

Eric cut across the lawn to join her.

"Locked pretty tight," he said, his voice breaking the spell.

With one last puzzled glance at the house, Lindsay turned to her husband. His expression somber, he crouched down to the sand, picked up a couple of small brown shells and threw them into the water. She wished he would talk to her, tell her what was troubling him.

"Honey, please talk to me, let me in—"

"I love you, you know," he interrupted. "Just let that be enough." Even crouching, his entire body seemed to sag, and his eyes held none of the roguish twinkle that used to be such a part of him.

Was his anguish due to some problem in their marriage he felt reluctant to discuss with her? But they'd talked openly about everything, including her anxiety-ridden childhood. Or was it something else?

Whatever it was, she'd give him the benefit of the doubt—at least until he recovered from his aunt's passing.

"Okay," she said. "We'll drop it. For now."

His relief was obvious. "Let's check into the motel and get something to eat."

"Eat first. I'm starved."

Just as Eric swung around to head down the dirt road, something in an upstairs window caught her eye. A subtle outline, as if someone were watching them.

"Honey …"

He finished the turn.

"What?"

Lindsay twisted in her seat and looked back at the window. Whatever she saw was gone.

"Nothing."

It was only the setting sun reflecting off the glass, creating distorted images that weren't really there.

Chapter Two

Minutes later, they entered Crosby, a former iron mining town spruced up with green awnings and antique stores. Lindsay caught a glimpse of Serpent Lake between Main Street's city blocks and thought how lucky the residents were to have a lake on one side of town and a forest on the other.

But at eight in the evening, the six-block downtown area was dark and deserted except for a convenience store with two gas pumps in front and a video rental place further down the street.

"Hope something is open," Lindsay said, scanning the buildings. A nice dinner and a glass of wine would be heaven after an entire day of traveling.

Lights brightened the inside of one cafe, but according to the sign, it was due to close in ten minutes. Maybe they could order something and take it to the motel.

Inside, the smell of grease and old cigarette smoke hung in the air. Two men in jeans and baseball caps sat at the counter, talking and laughing over slices of pie. A thin, wrinkled woman occupied a booth, her short white hair spiking in all directions, a pink quilted jacket hugging her emaciated body. A radio played country music, and a blackboard listed the day's specials. Most had been crossed out with chalk.

Eric and Lindsay took a booth by a window overlooking Main Street. A waitress about forty, in jeans and a sleeveless blouse, brought them water. *Shirley,* her nametag read. She recommended the hot beef sandwiches.

"Real mashed potatoes," she told them, patting her elaborately fashioned French twist hairstyle. "Peeled them myself. And we have fresh apple pie. Made that, too."

"Do we have time for all that?" Eric asked.

"Sure," Shirley said. "I got to clean up. Besides, I wouldn't throw you out."

One of the men at the counter looked up. "I wouldn't be too sure about that. She's got a mean right hand."

"You should know, George," Shirley said.

Both men laughed.

"You folks passing through?" Shirley asked, scribbling on her order pad

"We're here about some property I inherited," Eric told her.

"Really?" She arched her penciled eyebrows. "Ain't that nice. Where at?"

"Just out of town. From my aunt, Frida Peterson."

Everything went silent, even the conversation at the counter stopped.

The faint click of the diner's ventilation system switching on sounded like a bass drum in the sudden silence. Cool air blew on Lindsay from above.

Shirley stopped writing. "The old Peterson place?"

"You know it?" Eric said.

"I've heard of it," the waitress mumbled, glancing at the old woman.

The look they exchanged was strangely intense. The men at the counter dropped some change by their plates and left without speaking.

"Well, your dinner will be right up." No longer smiling, Shirley passed their orders to the kitchen, then became busy wiping the counter. The old woman rose to pay her bill, all the while staring at Eric and Lindsay. She didn't return their smiles.

"What happened?" Lindsay whispered.

Eric shrugged. "Guess it's closing time."

***

Lindsay was opening her car door when the old woman from the diner rushed over to them and grabbed her hand.

"What is it?" she asked.

The wrinkled eyes bored into her so intently that Lindsay was unable to look away. The old woman finally spoke, her dentures clicking in her thin face.

"Stay away from that house! Evil lives there."

Chapter Three

The one-story motel sat on the northwest shore of the lake, with all the rooms facing the water. Lindsay waited while Eric checked them in.

Evil lives there. What did that old lady mean?

Suddenly the trip caught up with her. Totally exhausted, she didn't want to think, didn't want to do anything but fall into bed and stretch out next to her husband's warm body.

From several hundred feet away, an outboard motor buzzed to life, then the sound faded as the boat sped up the lake. Even from the car, Lindsay could hear the waves gently lapping the shore.

Eric pulled in front of the door at the far end of the motel.

"To escape the noise," he said.

Lindsay glanced around the vacant lot; theirs was the only car. "What noise?"

"You never know who might check in." He jumped out of the car, opened the motel door, and began unloading the car.

She grabbed an armful, walked through the open door—and came to an abrupt halt.

Twin beds. Two individual beds separated by a solid oak night stand holding a bible and a green ceramic lamp. Each bed was neatly made, its own little world at a distance from the other.

"Twin beds?" She dropped her handbag and overnight case on the bed closest to the wall.

Eric was already digging through his suitcase. He said nothing, just kept busy until he found his pajama bottoms and disappeared into the bathroom. Lindsay grabbed her toothbrush and was about to follow him when the bathroom door closed—nearly in her face.

Taken aback, she sat on the bed.

The bathroom door opened a short while later and Eric, clad in pajama bottoms over his briefs, exited. Lindsay was astonished. He had never worn pajamas in the entire year they'd been married.

Avoiding her eyes, he climbed into bed.

"Honey, I'm beat," he said, busily arranging the top sheet over him, "and we have a lot to do tomorrow. Our appointment with the attorney is at nine, and we have to stop at the mortuary. I need to get some sleep."

"Of course." Lindsay rose to give him a quick kiss, but he clicked off his light and rolled over to face the wall.

At a total loss, Lindsay stared at his back.

Tension crackled in the air.

"Eric—" she began.

"Don't make a big deal out of nothing. I'm tired, that's all."

After an hour of lying in bed staring at the ceiling, Lindsay ran water for a bath. Instead of showering in the morning, perhaps a warm soak would relax her.

She lay back in the tub, her head resting against the blue-tiled wall. She breathed deeply, trying to ease the pressure in her chest, that old tightening she'd felt growing up with a vagabond mother, the creeping fear that snaked through every nerve in her body, taking over, crushing her so she couldn't eat or sleep. Something was threatening her marriage, and it was worse than her childhood, because this time, she had no idea what the threat was. Only that it was there, growing, just beyond her vision.

She had to get some answers, had to convince Eric to talk about the problem so they could fix it.

But was now the right time?

He must be exhausted from adjusting to the expanded territory at work, and, his aunt had just died. Though he hadn't seen her in years, he obviously thought a great deal of her. Coming back to his childhood home must be emotional for him, a time of memories, some good, some not so good. Growing up with two maiden aunts after his father died and his mother went to work couldn't have been easy for a young boy, and now she needed to support him in every way she could.

She'd wait until he settled his aunt's estate, then she'd insist on some answers.

***

When Lindsay woke the next morning, Eric was already dressed. He kept glancing at her as if bracing himself.

But today was going to be a long day for him, full of legalities and memories, so she wanted to make it easier for him. When she smiled, he brightened, and she caught a glimpse of the old Eric, a man of positive energy and charm.

After a quick breakfast at the bakery, they climbed narrow stairs in an old frame building to the attorney's office. From behind a cluttered oak desk, a stocky man with thick white hair rose and shook their hands.

"So sorry for your loss," Mr. Mathews said once they were seated. "Miss Frida was a fine woman. I was her attorney for years. Miss Berina's as well, before she passed on about forty years ago."

"I just have a vague memory of Aunt Berina," Eric told him. "She died when I was seven. That was about the second year I stayed with them."

"Your Aunt Frida was a wonderful woman," Mathews said. "She devoted her life to taking care of Miss Berina until the day of her death."

"What was wrong with Berina?" Lindsay asked. "Was she the oldest?"

"The youngest," Mathews said. "By a couple of years. And she was a beautiful woman, although she lived a secluded life. Some say she just wasted away."

"I never knew much about her," Eric said, "other than rumors about some kind of nervous breakdown. But no one in the family talked about it."

"Well, that's as it should be," Mathews said briskly, his tone closing further discussion. "Now, as I told you on the telephone, Miss Frida will be cremated, all according to her instructions. There's to be no service, then she wanted her ashes scattered in the lake."

"I thought she'd want to be buried with the family," Eric said.

"I was surprised as well." Mathews replied. "I'd be remiss if I didn't inform you that while scattering ashes in the lake isn't illegal at this time, it is considered a nuisance and not to be encouraged. Nevertheless, once the cremains are turned over to the family, all official responsibilities end. Do you understand?"

"Yes, thank you."

"Of course," Mathews continued, "if you must return to California before then, I'm to take care of it."

"We can stay a few extra days, can't we?" Eric asked Lindsay.

"Absolutely." Extra time away from work would be wonderful for him, she thought. Maybe he could finally relax.

"The estate has gone through probate and it's all ready for disbursement." Mathews cleared his throat. "Have you seen the property?"

"Just a quick look last evening," Eric replied. "The house was locked, of course."

"Mr. Mathews," Lindsay began. "The strangest thing happened." She paused and both men looked at her. "We stopped for dinner at the diner, and this old woman—"

Eric laughed. "You're not going to tell him about *that*, are you?"

"About what, Mrs. Peterson?"

She told the attorney about their reception in the diner after the people learned who they were, finishing with the old woman's warning. "'Evil lives there,' she said. It was creepy."

"You didn't take that seriously, did you?" Eric asked. "Even small towns have strange people wandering around jabbering nonsense." He glanced at Mathews as if seeking corroboration.

The attorney stiffened. Lindsay detected a slight reddening in his cheeks. Why would an attorney flush?

Mathews cleared his throat. "That they do," he said, bending down to search through files stacked on the floor. "Here we are." He pulled out a legal-size file. "You have a couple of decisions to make."

"Everything's in order, isn't it?" Eric asked.

"Certainly. Even after Miss Frida was moved to the nursing home ten years ago, she had periods of total lucidity. No problem there." Mathews opened a manila envelope and extracted some papers.

"As you know, you're the only heir, so there shouldn't be any challenges with the deed transfer. However," he paused, pulling off his glasses, "there's an unusual provision we have to address. Your aunt demanded that once she passed away, the house and all the associated buildings be destroyed by fire."

"No!" Lindsay cried, surprised at how much she already loved the house.

Eric frowned. "Burn it down? Why on earth would she want to do something like that?"

"It doesn't make sense," Lindsay said. "It's a little rundown, but the place is lovely. Or it could be with some TLC."

Mathews nodded. "It was indeed a showplace in its time." He paused. "You should know there's already a question as to the enforcement of that provision. As executor and as her attorney, I owe fiduciary loyalty to Miss Frida; however, I can't go beyond the boundary of the law."

"Meaning?" Eric asked.

"While I'm obligated to adhere to the terms of the will, I cannot do anything illegal." Mathews leaned back and folded his hands over his ample stomach. "That will was drafted thirty years ago, and laws have changed. We now have a fire ordinance prohibiting burning in the city's immediate area—especially a home and its contents. Toxic air pollutants, you understand, from lead, plastics, and other household materials. Ordinarily, we'd find some other way to destroy the property, which is technically going against the demand, so already we have a tort—a breach of contract of sorts. Before I decide how to proceed, I'd like to know your intentions regarding the house."

"We're thinking of using it as a vacation home," Eric told him. "I grew up here before my mother and I moved to California."

"Yes, I'm aware of that. I'm sure, as the descendant of one of Crosby's founding citizens, visiting here must bring back a lot of memories. However—"

"Founding citizens?" Lindsay broke in. While Eric had talked about his grandparents and some of the difficulties they'd faced while building a life in the winter's sub-zero temperatures, he'd never mentioned they had been prominent in the area.

"Indeed they were," Mathews said. "However, while it's a fine old house, almost a historical landmark, I wouldn't advise keeping it. You could raze the house and sell the land."

Lindsay frowned. "But I like the house." The thought of that lovely place being burned to the ground because of a whim of an old woman seemed outrageous.

Eric agreed. "Why would I want to destroy the house? I don't understand. Sure, it needs quite a bit of work, but it's in a prime location—far enough from the other lakefront homes to afford privacy, yet close enough to walk to town. And with the forest in back, it's ideal."

"I'm afraid that even though the Peterson trust held funds for maintenance, the house, as I'm sure you noticed, has fallen into some disrepair."

Mathews seemed embarrassed, Lindsay thought. Or was it something else?

"I, uh, had difficulties keeping someone and ten years is a long time."

"I understand," Eric said. "We'd expect to do some remodeling. Mind you, we haven't made any final decisions, but we'd like to know our options."

"Still, vacationing here would be quite a change from your California lifestyle," Mathews said. "Something you should consider."

Again he seemed flustered and Lindsay wondered why. He was obviously an experienced attorney. "Is there something you're not telling us, some reason we shouldn't keep the house?"

"No, no, nothing like that. I simply want you to consider what it would mean to keep the house intact." With an abrupt change of topic, he continued. "Would you like a formal reading of the will? I can check with Helen to schedule a time."

"That's not necessary," Eric told him. "If you don't mind, just give me the details now. I'm not sure of the financial status, especially with Aunt Frida in the nursing home so many years, but were there any funds left? In case we keep the house."

"The trust your grandparents left Crosby has helped fund many community improvements and we all get the benefit. And while there's not a large sum of money, there's enough, together with the bonds, to do some repairs to the property—within reason, of course. If you decide to follow through with Miss Frida's wishes and raze the house, you could rebuild. Or even sell the land if you don't wish to use it. Just let me know your decision as soon as you can."

Chapter Four

Downstairs, Eric and Lindsay decided to walk the three blocks to the mortuary. Traffic on Crosby's Main Street was sporadic, the few cars and RVs, many of them pulling boats, passing by at a slow speed. Minutes would pass before another vehicle drove by. Lindsay found the pace restful after living near an interstate in Southern California all her life.

"That old lady isn't the only strange one here," Lindsay said. "He didn't come out and say it, but I got the distinct impression Mr. Mathews didn't want us to keep the house."

Eric shrugged. "I doubt it's anything personal. As Aunt Frida's attorney, even with the new burn laws, he must perform his duty to her as much as possible."

"Miss Frida? Miss Berina? He sounded straight out of Tara, but we're too far north for that."

"What can I tell you? Small town, old habits. My grandfather was well-known in his day, president of the bank, and he helped build several roads around here." Eric grinned. "Didn't know you were so well-connected, did you?"

"Well, I'm certainly impressed. I didn't know I'd married a celebrity."

"Stick with me, kid," he teased, "and I'll show you lots of things. Important things like how to skip a rock in water, or how to dig for the best fishing worms. Bet you never knew that was an art, did ya?"

Delighted at Eric's lighthearted mood, Lindsay slipped her arm around him and drew close. He accepted the touch for a moment, then took a short step to the side, just enough out of reach for her to drop her arm. She stopped and stared at him in bewilderment.

"Honey …"

"Lindsay, please. Don't start again. I'm going through something I can't explain. Just have some patience."

"Talk to me, Eric. Maybe I can help. That's what married people do, you know. Discuss things and work them out."

Eric said nothing. In silence they crossed the street in front of the small newspaper office, Eric taking her arm like the courtly gentleman he'd always been—which made his aloof behavior all the more puzzling.

Was it another woman? She knew it was possible, but in the time she'd known him, he'd never betrayed her in any way. No matter the situation, she could always rely on his strength and honesty. If he'd fallen for someone else, he'd tell her.

"Mr. Mathews said your aunt Berina wasted away," she said, hoping to get him talking about his family, desperately wanting to recapture his former good spirits. "I bet it was over a lost love."

"I barely remember her. I didn't talk to her much because she always seemed so sad. She was good to me, though, and I loved her in my way."

"He said she'd been beautiful. Do you remember what she looked like?"

"Oh, tall and slim, I think, always kept her hair in one of those bun-things. I saw it down once, right before she went to bed, and it was long and fluffy. I don't remember if she was pretty, but she always smelled like lavender."

"Did either of your aunts ever marry?"

"I heard rumors that Aunt Frida had been engaged once, but I don't know what happened."

At the mortuary, the funeral director expressed his sympathy and assured them that he'd call when the cremains were ready.

Back on Main Street, Eric took Lindsay's arm. "You haven't seen our version of Nessie yet."

"Nessie?"

Eric smiled and took her arm. "You'll see."

They made a left and walked the two blocks to the city park that rimmed the lakefront road.

Fifty-year-old oaks and elms provided shade for the camping tents scattered on the lush green lawn.

An old pickup pulling a fishing boat was backing up next to a wooden dock.

But Lindsay's attention was drawn to a gigantic sea serpent statue reigning loftily from its concrete base set on a grassy area between the dock and swimming beach. Brightly colored in shades of yellow, red, and green, the fiberglass serpent stood at least twenty-feet high and was curled in a vertical 'w' about as long as it was tall.

"You said there were no poisonous snakes this far north," Lindsay said. "The idea for that must have come from somewhere."

"That's Kahnah'bek," Eric told her, grinning. "Native American legend says he lives in the lake. It's said that on magical occasions, he appears on the surface. Just think, our own little Nessie."

"And you expect me to vacation next to the water? No way."

"Oh, come on," he said, laughing, "Where's your sporting blood?"

"Right inside my body where it belongs, thank you very much. Not splattered all over by some sea monster."

"Don't worry. The baddest creature you'll find in this lake is a Northern Pike."

Warmed by the look he gave her, Lindsay decided to put their problems aside and enjoy the day with her husband. With his work schedule, they hadn't been able to spend much time together since their quick honeymoon in San Francisco.

At the Peterson house, they walked the grounds before unlocking the door, enjoying the fresh summer air.

"Oh, look!" Lindsay pointed to a black squirrel rushing down the trunk of a large oak, a smaller gray one in hot pursuit. The two raced across the lawn and disappeared up another tree.

"If you think that's great," Eric said, "just wait until evening when the deer come out to feed."

"This place is a living zoo."

"I wonder if the old motorboat is still here. Think I'll check before we tour the house." He headed for a garage-like structure on the water's edge.

Lindsay decided the house wasn't in as bad a shape as she'd first thought. The overall structure appeared pretty straight, and the window facings seemed in good repair. Maybe all it needed were a few nails to tighten things up and a coat of paint. Even the two dormer windows in the attic looked okay. They could divide the attic into rooms. Eric could have one for his computer, and she could have one for her painting.

She had painted all her life, doodling and sketching while growing up, burying herself in paper instead of playing with other kids, and as an adult, she had shown her work in a Palm Springs gallery. When the owner decided to retire, Eric provided the backing for her to purchase the gallery. While it was successful, her own work had suffered. Mired in administrative affairs, her creative nature had faded until she no longer painted, but now, studying the attic windows overlooking the lake, she felt sure her artistic side would flourish again—if she could get her marriage back on track. If any place on earth could help, she felt that here, in the serenity of Eric's childhood home, whatever was troubling him would surely lessen and disappear.

Without knowing how it had happened, Lindsay realized how drawn she felt toward everything on the property. The beautiful old screened porch, even though sagging now, provided a magical place to sit in the evening and read or to listen to the frogs and fish jumping for insects. And since she loved the water, they could build another gazebo next to the water, right in the same spot where the first one used to be. Looking over the property, the house, the rich green lawn with the full-leafed maples and oak trees filled with birds and squirrels, it all seemed to call to her and fill her heart with joy. She no longer felt the sadness from before, just a peace and contentment, as if she were coming home after a long, tiring vacation.

Eric was still puttering around the boathouse, so she climbed the wooden porch steps and stepped carefully over the warped boards. She didn't know anything about carpentry, but she thought a little work could make it good as new. She found an ideal place for a swing and envisioned plants hanging from the beams.

She cupped her hands to peer through a grimy front window. Heavy drapes blocked the view. Idly, she tried one of the double doors, twisting the brass knob, only to find that it turned smoothly. The heavy wooden door fell open as easily as if someone on the other side were inviting her in.

She stepped into a wood-paneled entryway that led to a darkened stairway directly ahead. The door closed behind her.

Lindsay paused to give her eyes time to adjust to the gloom. The house sighed, and an aromatic scent filled the hallway, a light spicy fragrance she had smelled before but couldn't name. She felt a stirring of air near her, the gentle warmth surrounding her, enveloping her like a lover's caress.

Chapter Five

Suddenly the front door flew open and hit the wall with a loud thud. Eric stood in the doorway rubbing his shoulder.

"I'll have a dislocated shoulder if I have to do that very often." He turned to her with a puzzled frown. "How'd you get in?"

"Opened just fine for me. I guess you don't have the magic touch."

"That's odd. Last night it was locked so tight you'd think the CIA was storing secret documents in here." He examined the door, then the lock. "Must be some kind of quirk. We'll get a locksmith out here just to make sure, although I doubt there's any reason to worry."

"Did you smell anything when you came in?"

"Yeah. A musty, closed-up-old-house." He glanced around the foyer. "See the intricate woodwork? Grandpa spared no expense building this house for Grandma. It's a bit dusty, but it's just like I remember."

Lindsay smiled at the satisfaction in his voice.

"I hope the rest of the house isn't in too bad a shape. Come on." He led her through a high archway on the left. "This was the parlor, reserved for guests during my grandparents' day. My aunts weren't so formal."

Lindsay noticed the scent had disappeared. "That smell was pretty strong." She glanced back at the foyer.

"Let's get some fresh air in here. And some light." Eric pulled the heavy gold drapes. Clouds of dust filled the air. Coughing, he opened the windows and shafts of sunlight brightened the room.

"It's lovely!" Larger than their living room back home, Lindsay thought it felt even more spacious because of the high ceilings. A rock fireplace with a rich mahogany mantle took up the center wall, and on the floor, clear plastic runners stretched over a faded oriental rug that partly covered an oak floor. Yellowed sheets covered a few pieces of furniture.

She couldn't resist peeking at the overstuffed chairs and a sofa, all made of yellow damask. And in the corner, a highly-polished Victrola cabinet stood with some old seventy-eight records still stacked in the bottom. They must be worth a fortune.

"What in the world is that?" she asked, pointing to four wall ducts, each about fifteen inches square, mounted against the baseboard.

"That's for the oil furnace in the basement."

"Oil furnace?"

"It has to be filled once a month. If we keep the house, we'll convert to gas."

The parlor opened to a dining room just as spacious as the first room. A dusty chandelier, its crystal prisms draped in cloth, hung over a partially-covered mahogany dining table large enough to seat twelve. An elaborately carved buffet stood on one side of the table, and a matching sideboard on the other.

"Oh, look. Aren't they beautiful?"

Eric smiled. "Told you."

Lindsay paused at the large bay window to gaze at the woods edging the overgrown lawn at the back of the house. How wonderful to take meals in a room overlooking a forest crowded with trees, shrubs, and wildlife.

And how familiar it seemed. The magnificent red oak standing at the edge of the lawn, its heavy lower branch stretching to the west, the clusters of white birch, all mature now, rising above wild pin cherry bushes. When she spotted a towering black ash topping the thicket at nearly sixty feet, she felt an overwhelming joy and wanted to dash out the back door and embrace that crooked old tree's furrowed gray trunk as if greeting an old friend.

A stirring of warm, vibrant air whispered in her ear, a slight humming sound, so low it was almost a vibration. All her senses were tuned to the sound, and she turned, expecting to see him standing next to her, sharing her memories, bringing them alive again.

From across the room Eric slammed a sideboard drawer shut. Startled at the sudden sound, Lindsay blinked—and found herself standing alone at the dining room window. The same bewildering grief she'd felt yesterday began to grow, squeezing her heart until she could barely take a breath. Her eyes moistened.

She wiped a teardrop with her finger and stared in puzzlement. Who was the 'him' she'd expected to see? And what, for heaven's sake, would cause her to think such fanciful thoughts or feel such strong emotions? Perplexed, she looked at the tree again, but it was simply a nice tree in the forest.

What was wrong with her?

"Did you tell me about a special tree in the back of the house?" she asked Eric.

"A special tree? Of course not."

"You didn't build a tree house or anything?"

Ignoring her question, he headed for the kitchen. "Let's see the rest of the house."

Lindsay glanced once more out the window, then followed.

After the exceptional condition of the parlor and dining room, Lindsay felt disappointed at the warped cabinet doors and café curtains underneath the sink instead of a cabinet. A big rust spot ringed the drain. She wouldn't have been surprised to see an old water pump mounted on the rim.

A hallway led them to another front room across from the parlor.

"We used this as the family room."

The windows, like those in the parlor, opened onto the porch and provided a view of the sparkling blue expanse of the lake. A pot-bellied stove, with dull nickel decorating the black iron, was mounted on a brick pad in the corner. All it needed was a little bit of polish to make it sparkle. Lindsay decided it would make quite a conversation piece, and she was even more determined than ever to keep this lovely home.

The stairwell opened to three bedrooms and a bathroom on the second floor, with a landing spacious enough for a comfortable chair and bookcases by the window overlooking the lake.

Unfortunately the bathroom was as outdated as the kitchen. Instead of the familiar porcelain tank behind the seat, two pipes led to a boxlike object mounted on the wall above.

"It's an old-fashioned water closet," Eric told her, pointing to a long slim rod on the left side. "You pull this to flush."

Lindsay frowned. She could make do with an older kitchen but that bathroom had to go.

They continued on to the attic where partial walls for a small bedroom had been fashioned under the sloping roof. There was a twin bed, the bare mattress under a dulled brass headboard still in place. A scarred dressing table stood against one wall with a flower-painted ceramic pot and lid next to it.

"That's a chamber pot," Eric explained. "I imagine the outhouse is still in the woods."

"Good God!"

Eric grinned. "I can just see you half asleep on that thing in the middle of the night."

"And they call those the good old days?" But despite everything, Lindsay loved the place.

The rest of the attic held unused furniture and boxes spilling over with discards, but Lindsay was drawn to the front windows. She gazed through the dusty panes to the serene lake below.

The sun rode high above, casting its shimmering reflection on the water. From her vantage point, she could see down the water's edge to the motel and the park with a swimming area. Several boats were scattered on the lake, and she watched as one fisherman hooked something, his rod bending as he reeled it in.

Slowly, the brightness of the attic dimmed, as if a shadow had slipped in front of the sun. She became aware of a faint, spicy scent with a hint of cloves, the same fragrance she'd smelled when she first entered the house.

It grew stronger.

Thinking that perhaps it came from outside, she unlocked the window and raised it, amazed at how easily it opened. She inhaled deeply. The air was fresh, so the scent wasn't coming from outside.

"There it is again," she said. "Smell it?"

"Umm," Eric murmured, absorbed in the contents of one of the boxes stacked against the wall.

A slight breeze ruffled Lindsay's hair, touching her face in a light kiss. Her skin tingled and the hairs on her arms stiffened. An incredible warmth and excitement spread through her as if all the all the physical pleasures she'd been denied were centered right there in the attic, just waiting for her. Her nipples hardened. She turned toward the stir of air, reveling in the familiar scent, closing her eyes and lifting her face to the feather-touch against her lips.

Eric came up behind her. "Smells pretty rank up here," he said. "It's a good thing you opened the window."

Lindsay snapped out of her reverie, annoyed at Eric's interruption. Her cheeks were hot and she felt flushed. To her astonishment, her panties were moist. Flustered, she turned from the window, hoping Eric wouldn't notice anything amiss.

He tugged open the other window. "Maybe there's a dead mouse or a squirrel in the walls. Let's get some lunch and let it air out up here."

They descended the stairs, Eric leading the way. "I'm glad to get out of there," he said. "There's something about that attic I don't like."

Lindsay paused to look over her shoulder. There was something about the attic all right, something oddly physical. But she wasn't repelled. Puzzled perhaps, and curious, maybe even intrigued.

She had no idea what had just happened to her in that attic, but something had, something she couldn't explain.

Chapter Six

"Ready for some lunch?" Eric asked. "The coffee and doughnuts this morning didn't last long."

Lindsay nodded, thinking about the house.

What did happen in that attic? How could she have been so affected by something as insubstantial as a breath of air?

It had to be the excitement of inheriting the house and the possibility of a different lifestyle. Living by the water had always been a dream of hers, but with the prices in California, it was something she had never thought possible. Vacations on a nice lake would be a joy, then later, they could retire there permanently.

So it wasn't so unusual; she had heard of people becoming aroused at the oddest times—just before a battle and even after a funeral.

And maybe it was the house. Maybe in combination with weather conditions—a high or low pressure or a change in the barometer.

Eric took the long way and drove down Main Street, starting at the one-story hospital and clinic bordering the forest on the eastern edge of town. Lindsay noted with appreciation nature's different colors around her, the pink flowering crab tree, the deep blue water, the luxurious green grass, so different from the desert beiges surrounding Palm Springs. She lowered the window and breathed deeply.

"All this fresh air, I hope my lungs don't collapse from shock."

Eric rolled down his window and rested his elbow on the sill.

"Don't worry. The human body can adapt to almost anything. It's a growing lilt to your speech or a sudden fondness for Lutefisk—" he pronounced it with a Scandinavian accent, sing-songing the syllables—"that would give me pause."

"Surely, that can't be something to eat."

"Dried cod preserved in lye," he explained. "My grandparents used to store it in barrels. When you're ready to eat it, you skin it, take the bones out and then boil it."

"Sounds right tasty to me."

Eric laughed. "It's an acquired taste, but one you should try while we're here."

"I can't wait."

His cell phone rang and it was Mark, his field manager in California, upset over the latest crisis.

While Eric tried to calm him down, Lindsay stared out the window and tried to force down the irritation that bubbled inside. Wouldn't they even allow him some time while on a bereavement leave?

They passed the small grocery store, and Lindsay spotted an older man sweeping the parking lot with a push broom, his cap shading his ruddy complexion from the sun. Two elderly women strolling by stopped to chat.

Everything looked so picturesque, and people took time to enjoy their lives. Before her experience in the house, she would have loved to live here.

She frowned. No mater how she tried to rationalize, what had happened in the attic nagged at her. It just wasn't normal.

And what about that tree?

Inside the diner, they sat at one of the chrome tables. A small circular fan on the counter pushed the stale air through the screened door. A couple of grey-haired women sat in one of the four booths, but most of the lunch crowd had left.

Lindsay ordered the lunch special, a tuna-salad sandwich with a cup of hamburger soup. Eric decided on a cheeseburger with fries.

"You know," he said, pouring catsup on his fries, "driving through town, I'm reminded of a time long ago, a way of life that's fifty years in the past. Here, people actually know their neighbors and care about them. Can you imagine such a thing?"

Lindsay sweetened her tea and thought about the spicy scent in the house. It had a vague familiarity like a beloved old picture, but just as she was close to naming it, it eluded her.

But her body had reacted, softening with desire and welcoming the scent.

Evil, the old lady had said.

"—and I can't wait," he was saying.

"What?" Lindsay blinked.

"The house. I didn't think I'd ever be back here, except for a visit, but now I can't wait. We should have a contractor look at it, get an idea what the remodeling will cost."

Contractor?

"First, though," Eric went on between bites of burger, "we'll have to make sure we get the place." He wiped mustard from his mouth. "I can't imagine what possessed Aunt Frida. True, she was always a little eccentric, but this is just plain weird. Maybe I can challenge the will based on incompetence or something."

"Slow down." Lindsay put down her spoon. "We're moving much too fast. We haven't decided we want it."

"Of course we want it. I didn't know there was any question."

She took one of Eric's curly fries, examined it then put it into her mouth and chewed.

"Why the hesitation?" he asked. "I thought you liked it."

"I do," she said slowly. "But there are ... things to consider."

"What things? And why the change in attitude? If it's a question of the will, well, I bet Mathews can find a way around it."

"It's not just that ..."

"What is it, then?" he prodded.

"What that old woman said bothers me."

"Lindsay," he said, sighing. "I thought we'd settled that."

"I know, but something about her eyes ..."

Eric studied her a moment. "Okay, what's the problem? I don't understand your reluctance."

Lindsay didn't know what to say. She saw the excitement in his eyes at the thought of owning his childhood home and realized the tiny lines around his nose and mouth had relaxed. Being here was good for him—which made her doubts even more of a dilemma.

"You know the kids would love a place like that," Eric pressed on. His son and daughter-in-law lived in Denver with their three-year-old daughter, and Lindsay's son was single, on active duty in Norfolk, Virginia. "With a private beach and a place to fish, why it's a perfect place for grandchildren. What's not to like?"

"I didn't say I didn't like it." Avoiding his eyes, Lindsay stirred her tea, jabbing the ice chunks with her straw.

"Obviously there's something you don't like," Eric said, his voice sounding strained. "And I don't understand what it is. I'm not asking you to move here permanently, just vacation here."

In the two years they'd known each other, they'd never had a serious disagreement, always managing to talk over everything and working it out—except for the past month or so that Eric had been distant. He'd refused to discuss it, always dismissing her concerns as imagination.

Imagination.

A wife always knew when her husband's attitude toward her changed, but she'd decided it was due to his work pressures, then the news about his aunt's death.

If he thought her concerns were imaginary before, he'd think her concerns about the attic were unreasonable. He'd be right. Hesitating to return to that house because she'd become physically aroused in the attic sounded preposterous even to her.

Not knowing what to say, she took his hand across the table.

"Please, honey, let's not argue. Let's just wait and see what happens. Mr. Mathews might not be able to overturn the will and then all of this would be pointless."

Eric pulled his hand away and sat back, leaving half his burger on his plate. "It sounds as if you hope that's what happens. I can't believe you'd want to deny me my grandparents' home."

Lindsay fought tears. How had this discussion become so ugly so quickly? "I'm not trying to deny you anything," she said quietly.

"Then what's the problem?"

"What about other places we'd talked about visiting on vacations? The east coast, or Niagara Falls and Mount Rushmore."

"We can do that too. I just want my grandparents' home, the house I lived in for several years. Why should that be so difficult to understand?"

She said nothing. How could she explain something so elusive as a feeling?

Eric threw down his napkin and stood. "I'm ready to leave. Are you?"

Silently and not touching, they paid the bill and left the diner.

They spent the afternoon exploring some of the antique shops along Main Street, each so polite to the other that Lindsay wanted to scream. After a quick dinner, they returned to the motel to watch TV. Lindsay tried to read but was too upset over the growing tension between them. All evening she debated about being honest with Eric, but felt too ashamed. The more she thought about it and the longer she was away from the house, the more she decided she was being foolish.

She needed to talk to her husband, to reconnect, but she wasn't sure how to reach out to him. Should she say she was sorry? That after getting him so upset she'd simply changed her mind? That seemed even worse.

The silence stretched between them.

Chapter Seven

Eric moved to the chair, then snapped on the TV. She glanced down at her book but had no idea what she'd read. Some time later, mumbling something about taking a walk, Eric left the room without asking if she'd like to come along.

What was happening to her perfect marriage?

She had waited all her life for someone like Eric, a sensitive, caring man who always seemed to have her best interests at heart. Now that she had found him, she couldn't drive him away. She had to talk to him, to make up for the hurt feelings she had caused.

Hoping the right words would come to her, she turned off the TV and opened the door, surprised to discover it had grown dark.

Lindsay crossed the narrow driveway. The floodlight cast a yellowed light on the motel's dock, and she stepped onto the wooden planks. Chained to a piling, a ten-foot aluminum boat bobbed gently in the water, and a red Sea-Doo sat next to a two-seat paddle wheeler.

Eric sat at the end of the dock smoking a cigar, a habit he'd acquired after giving up cigarettes almost ten years ago. She knew he was upset; he only lit up when he felt angry or frustrated.

He said nothing, just continued to smoke and stare out over the water, but he made room for her. Silently, she sat down beside him.

In the distance, a couple of slow-moving white lights floated low in the middle of the lake.

"What are those?" she asked quietly.

Eric didn't immediately answer and the silence stretched between them. Lindsay waited, holding her breath. Wasn't he going to talk to her?

He finally sighed. "Running lights on fishing boats."

Lindsay felt like throwing her arms around him in relief, but she kept her tone calm to match his. "People fish at night?"

"Some of the best fishing is done after dark."

"What kind?" She didn't really care, but at least he was talking. They could work through anything as long as they talked.

"Oh, sunfish, walleye, and crappies."

"Croppies?"

"Best pan fish around. Maybe one of the restaurants will have some you can try."

"That would be great."

Headlights by the park caught their attention and they watched as a pickup truck swung around to guide a boat-trailer into the lake. After the slap of the boat hitting the water, two men got out and cranked something on the trailer and did a few other things she couldn't quite make out, then got back into the truck and pulled it over to the side of the road to park. Under the floodlights by the dock, they carried some fishing gear to the boat. The starting engine sounded like a giant swarm of monster mosquitoes and soon the boat glided to the middle of the lake. It headed east. Gentle waves from the wake slapped the dock pilings. They watched until the lights disappeared around the curve of the lake and the water was still again.

"Where's the Peterson house from here?" she asked.

He indicated the northern shore. "Down that way, just before that bend. Right now it just looks like a black space with no lights."

Lindsay peered into the darkness but could see nothing but a patch of black.

"Tell me about your aunts," she said, mainly to keep him talking.

"What do you want to know?"

"Oh, just anything you remember. Going there, what it was like living with them."

Eric threw his cigar and a glowing amber arc fell into the water.

"After Dad's accident," he began, "Mom had to go to work and she worried about me being alone all summer. I think I was six. My grandparents died the year before, so I stayed with my aunts. Frida was the oldest, and since neither ever married, she took care of Berina. Berina was frail, a bit other-worldly, I found out later. I just knew that sometimes her eyes looked vacant, as if she weren't really there. She died the next year. I later heard whispers about both of them but I never saw anything wrong."

"What kind of whispers?"

"Something about them having delusions or not being quite right. Oh, occasionally one of them would come out with something strange, but I didn't pay attention."

"Strange in what way?" Lindsay held her breath.

"I don't remember. I was too busy with swimming and fishing. I got a chance to be Huckleberry Finn and I loved it." His voice trailed off.

"Go on," Lindsay encouraged, recognizing the nostalgia in his tone. She knew what it felt like to long for something, to always want something out of reach.

"I was ten or eleven when Mom found her job and we moved to California," Eric continued. "I tried to visit Aunt Frida when I could, but I got involved in Scouts and a paper route. Then girls. I really felt bad that I didn't visit as often as I should have."

Lindsay took his arm and leaned her head on his shoulder, drawing on his warmth and taking comfort in having him next to her. She stared out over the water. How she loved this man who had given her back her life, who'd believed in her and encouraged her to follow her heart with the gallery. How could she possibly prevent him from his dream of taking possession of his childhood home?

She couldn't. For her husband, she had to overcome any hesitation she might feel and give back to him.

"Honey, I'm so sorry for today. Let's call Mr. Mathews tomorrow and tell him we want the house."

He was silent for a long moment. Then, his voice soft, he asked, "Why the sudden change?"

"Because I like the house, but most of all, I love you."

"Are you sure? I don't want you to do this if you have reservations."

"I was just being silly. Actually, it'll be fun fixing it up. And I can't wait to learn to fish. Can we shop for a pontoon?"

"Sure we will. We'll even get one with a potty, just for you." His voice became animated, gaining back some of the excitement he'd had earlier that day. "I have a great idea. Why don't we take another couple of weeks and move here for the summer? I'll take my vacation early and you could call Julia at the gallery." He paused a moment, then continued his thoughts, even more animated that before. "We can make a quick trip home, lease the condo, and pick up what you and I need to work this summer. What do you think?"

"Only one problem."

"What's that?" he asked, his tone wary again.

"We have to get a new bed. The one in the master bedroom looked old enough that your grandparents probably used it."

Laughing, Eric stood and helped her up. "We'll call Mathews in the morning to make the arrangements. It'll be great being back in the house."

Heading back to the motel room with Eric, Lindsay glanced back at the lake and at the black spot where Eric had said the house stood.

A cool breeze touched her face, lighter than a feather, but she shivered. While sitting next to Eric on the dock, moving in had seemed like a great idea.

Now she wasn't so sure.

Chapter Eight

Early the next morning, they checked with Mathews.

"It's looking good, so I don't foresee any problems," he told them. "I'll be meeting with the judge in a few days, but after speaking with him on the phone, I think you can safely assume the house will be yours. I'll send a fax after the decision, just let me know when you return."

The notice was waiting for them in their California attorney's office.

"The court agreed it was in the public's best interest to keep the house intact," Mathews had written, "so you now have full ownership of your ancestral home." As they'd discussed in his office, he'd also oversee home inspections and would hire maintenance and cleaning crews.

Three weeks later, after leasing their California condo for the summer, Eric backed the small rental truck into the lake house driveway. With their Prius attached to a tow bar on back, the caravan spread across the dirt road to the forest behind the house.

Birds in the maple and oak trees took flight and squirrels chattered at the intrusion.

Before unloading Eric's computer desk and Lindsay's art table plus a multitude of boxes, they walked around the property to check the work they'd commissioned.

According to what Lindsay was seeing today, Mathews had done an excellent job. Overgrown shrubs had been trimmed and dead limbs removed from the trees. New black shutters on all the windows highlighted the house's crisp white paint, and in the front, carpenters had replaced and widened the porch steps and added scrolled iron rails.

"What a difference." Eric was right behind her. "Now it's looking like the home I remember."

Hearing the catch in his voice, Lindsay slipped her arm through his. When away from the house, she'd questioned her decision, but now, Eric's happiness made it all worthwhile. With each mile they'd driven from California, he'd relaxed more and more, and when they crossed into Minnesota, he actually broke out in old bawdy songs from college. She'd laughed and tried to sing along with him. And when they pulled up to the house, she had been so glad to see the old place she almost broke down in tears.

What was it about this house that so mesmerized her? She had never felt that way about any other place, and heaven knew she'd lived in plenty of different houses and apartments. She felt such peace here. Comfort. Almost a welcome home.

Why she should sense such feelings, especially after what she'd experienced in the attic, she couldn't explain, but Eric's happiness made it all worthwhile.

Strolling the property, they paused to gaze at the water. "Just look at it, honey," Lindsay said. "I never thought I'd be living on a lake, especially such a beautiful one."

Today the cerulean water sparkled with golden reflections of the sun. The air felt heavier and moist and was alive with the buzzing of horseflies and mosquitoes. Perspiration drops beaded Lindsay's forehead and around her bra. She slapped a mosquito on her damp neck.

Eric smiled.

"Humidity gets pretty thick here in late summer, you know. Doesn't usually last more than a few days, but you just might want to turn around and head back to the desert."

"No way. Moist air will be great for my complexion, especially after living all my life in dry heat."

Arm in arm they climbed the porch steps and entered the house through new oak and glass double-doors.

Inside, the rooms smelled like lemon oil from the cleaning products, and on her tour, Lindsay couldn't detect the elusive spicy scent she had smelled before. The oak floors gleamed. Satin drapes in soft gold graced the squeaky-clean windows. New covers concealed the damask furniture. Even the wallpaper had been scrubbed.

"Oh my God, I don't believe it," Lindsay said, stepping through to the new kitchen.

Where warped cabinets and a rusty old sink with exposed pipes stood before, everything was now stainless steel and granite. New oak cabinets and a double-door refrigerator graced the kitchen. Someone had even placed a little round breakfast table with two chairs in the corner.

"It's like a new house," Lindsay exclaimed. "Later we can remodel the bathroom and get a new gazebo by the beach where the old one used to be."

Eric laughed. "Whoa, tiger. I have to make sure my business doesn't suffer before we do anything else."

Inside the fridge, a bottle of Dom Perignon stood, a card and a red ribbon tied around the neck.

"Welcome," Mathews had written. "May you find joy in your home."

"How thoughtful," Lindsay said. "We can have some tonight to celebrate."

Just as he was unloading sacks of groceries into the fridge, he paused and looked at her with a puzzled frown.

"What makes you think there used to be a gazebo? I don't ever remember seeing one here."

Lindsay shrugged. "Must have seen it in an old photo."

The rest of the day passed in a flurry of unloading the truck and returning it, then emptying the boxes of necessities. Eric placed his office furniture in the third bedroom instead of the attic.

"It stinks up there," he told Lindsay. "I just don't like it."

Although she didn't understand his aversion, she loved the thought of having the entire space as a studio where she could play music while painting and wouldn't have to worry about disturbing him. She also wanted to get some comfortable furniture, perhaps an overstuffed chair or sofa, so she could take short breaks instead of coming downstairs.

That evening, she stepped onto the front porch. Eric sat in the glider they'd picked up at a used furniture place and she eased down beside him. Her hair hung in her face and her cotton blouse stuck to her damp skin. She yawned.

"Some vacation this is turning out to be. I'm more tired than if I'd worked all week."

"The hard part's done now. And it'll be worth it. Just look at that moon."

A breeze from the lake rustled the leaves on the maple trees. Crickets chirped and mosquitoes whined. In the night, the lake stretched out like a black silky ribbon, and the full moon rose high in the sky, creating a kaleidoscope of indigo and gray patterns as it passed through the night clouds. Strips of silver reflections shimmered on the water.

"It's beautiful here," Lindsay said, burrowing close to Eric. "And so peaceful. But I'm too tired to appreciate it."

Eric kissed her forehead. "Poor baby. I'm all sympathy."

"I can hear how sympathetic you are. If I didn't know better, I'd say I married a heartless bastard."

"Hmmm, maybe I'd better persuade you to keep me around."

"You could try."

Eric brushed her lips, more like a brother than a husband. Instead of allowing herself to feel hurt, she decided to approach the problem in a different way. If she showed him how much she loved him, was patient and understanding, maybe she could help him overcome whatever was troubling him. Then they could begin their new lives together.

"Mmmm," Lindsay murmured. "We should christen our new home like we did our apartment."

Eric drew back. Then, as if shrugging off doubts, he pulled her to her feet. "Let's go upstairs."

In the bedroom, Lindsay pulled off the blankets on the new bed and they fell onto the crisp sheets together.

When he kissed her, sliding his tongue into her mouth, Lindsay closed her eyes and tightened her arms around him. This was where she was the happiest, melted against her husband with his arms around her. He kissed her neck and gently sucked her earlobe, caresses that had always sent tingles along her spine.

But now, she felt ... nothing.

Slowly, he unbuttoned her blouse and kissed the skin above her breasts. Lindsay helped him strip off her bra, then she lay back and sighed, waiting for the delicious sensation of his warm mouth on her breast.

But something was wrong.

She felt the gentle sucking pressure of his lips on her nipple. But nothing else. She felt apart, almost as if she were standing at a distance and watching.

This had never happened before. She'd always responded to Eric, had loved feeling his body pressed against hers, had always gloried in their lovemaking.

So what was wrong now?

This was Eric, the man she loved more than life itself. She couldn't let this happen. If she tried harder, it would work. Wrapping her arms around his neck, she kissed him and ground her hips into his.

Eric paused over her nipples, gently tonguing and sucking each pink nub.

Desperately wanting to respond, she opened to him, urging him close to her, welcoming the sensuous feel of his body pressed against hers. He rested his weight on his elbows, and she rejoiced in his warmth and the security of his arms.

It was going to be okay. She could get through this. If she didn't feel the sexual lust she'd hoped, that was okay. She would just relax and wouldn't force it.

She slid her hand to his groin to caress him, but he changed position slightly so that she couldn't touch him. He seemed to renew his efforts at pleasing her, running his lips and tongue over her breasts, then lower, to her navel, then back up to the hollow of her neck.

She wanted to love him, to give him as much pleasure as he was trying to give her. She kissed him on the ear, gently sucking on the soft lobe, and ran her hands over his buttocks. She reached around to caress him, to capture the warm hardness that had always thrilled her before.

He was flaccid.

A cold wave of shock washed over her. Didn't she arouse him at all?

She kissed him again, a little more deeply, a little more urgently.

A loud clanging noise sounded from somewhere downstairs.

"What's that?" she asked.

"Probably the pipes."

Just as they kissed again, the noisy racket increased and reverberated up the stairway and throughout the house. Heavy thuds followed, sounding like a giant hitting the house with a colossal hammer.

They sprang apart and sat up.

"Good God." Lindsay held her blouse over her breasts.

Eric nearly leapt out of bed. "I'll check it out."

They trailed the sound to the kitchen and flipped on the lights. A large puddle of water was spreading on the floor in front of the sink and when Eric threw open the cupboard doors and crouched down, he was drenched by water spraying from the drainpipe. Lindsay ran to get some towels, dropping one on the floor and handing the other one to Eric.

"Oh hell! I have to turn off the water." He turned off the water under the sink and grabbed a flashlight. After he went outside, the clanking gradually decreased until it was a dull thud. Lindsay mopped up the water and waited.

Hoping the noise would stop, she fixed coffee for both of them and sat down to wait, but it continued, a light sound barely audible. But she could still hear it.

After about twenty minutes, she wandered outside and met him returning from the brick pump house.

"Did you find the problem?"

"No, damn it."

Back in the kitchen she handed him a cup of coffee. "What do you think happened?"

He brushed off the dirt from his face and clothes, then eased onto a chair.

"I don't know, but something might be wrong with the pump or the well. That knocking sounded like it came from somewhere underground."

"Can you fix it?"

"That's a major project, way beyond me. They'll probably have to dig up half the lawn to fix that old well. Hell, it's been around since the house was built.

How about some of that Jim Beam and Coke? I could use it tonight."

She mixed the drink and he gulped it down.

"Another one?" she asked. He rarely drank, only having a couple of drinks when they went out to a nice place for diner or a cold beer after yard work.

Eric sipped his second drink. "I'll call Mathews in the morning. Of all things to happen. New wells can run thousands of dollars and that'll sure put a dent into our funds. If that happens, we'll have to cut our vacation time short and head back home."

The house suddenly became quiet. Even the crickets no longer chirped.

"Hear that?" she asked.

"What? I don't hear anything."

"It stopped! Maybe that's a good sign. Maybe it won't be so bad after all," Lindsay said. "After all, it worked fine all of those years for your grandparents and aunts."

"Yeah, but look how long the place has been empty. Who knows that could've happened in that time." He held up his glass. "Fix me another, would you? Damn, I guess you were right about this place. Maybe I shouldn't have jumped at it after all."

She mixed another drink and handed him the glass. "Now that we're in," she said, looking around the newly scrubbed kitchen, "I'm loving the homey feel of the place."

Although outdated, she had begun to enjoy the comfortable feel of the large room—the soft golden walls with the apples and pears wallpaper, the shelves on the walls holding old mason jars and cookbooks from the Lutheran church's Ladies Auxiliary. Even the freshly washed ruffled curtains looked just right, something she never thought she'd tolerate for a moment. It all felt homey, somehow, and comfortable, as if she were right where she belonged.

"Ah ha! I knew thish, *this*," he repeated carefully, "old place ..." His words trailed off and he grinned. "Shouldn'ta had that lash drink. Been awhile."

"Well my goodness," Lindsay said with a grin. "Are you a little tipsy?"

"Reckon so."

"C'mon, big boy." Lindsay pulled him to a standing position. "Let's get you into bed."

Eric grinned agreeably and arm in arm, they climbed the steps. Upstairs, he stripped off his clothes, dropped onto the bed and promptly fell asleep. Lindsay got him under the covers and within a few moments he was snoring softly. She quickly checked the house, making sure the doors were locked, then undressed and cuddled next to him, tucking the blankets around both of them.

The house seemed to sigh and the air shifted around her. The upstairs landing floorboards creaked as if someone were walking, but she wasn't afraid. She knew from locking up that no one was in the house. It was simply the sounds of the old house settling.

Just as she was drifting off to sleep, the spicy scent wafted gently to her, something familiar lying just underneath the furniture oil. A subtle aroma, yet something her senses recognized and welcomed. A kitchen spice? And perhaps something else she couldn't quite name. But she didn't care.

Somehow, the scent comforted her.

She slept.

Chapter Nine

A home inspector and a well-driller contractor spent the next morning testing the water system, and no irregularities were found.

After the last workman left, Eric and Lindsay sat at the kitchen table with some coffee.

"I don't understand it," Eric said. "Everything's working fine."

"Well thank goodness for that." Lindsay stirred a sweetener into her own cup. "Maybe now we can think about remodeling the bathroom. That pull chain toilet has to go."

"What's the matter?" he teased. "Don't you like roughing it? At least you don't have to visit the privy in the woods."

"That'll be the day."

Suddenly, Eric and the kitchen grew smaller and smaller until they faded completely, but she wasn't alarmed. Instead, it seemed natural, as if she were watching a home movie and one scene faded out so the next could begin. She was outside in the night, wearing a long robe, tromping along a dirt path behind the house carrying a bulky flashlight. The outhouse, discreetly tucked behind pine trees was just a few feet ahead.

She'd sure be glad when the new bathroom would be installed. Papa said if everything went right, it would be installed next week and she couldn't wait.

She wouldn't let him know how excited she was, though. Other than her courtesy answers, she'd vowed she wouldn't speak to him until he let her cut and style her hair in the short elfin style or even the poodle cut so popular with all the girls.

It was the only way; one didn't argue with Papa. His word was law. She just hoped he'd give in soon; she didn't know how long she could keep up the angry façade. She'd nearly smiled today when his booming Swedish voice teased and cajoled her again.

"Honey?" Eric asked, looking at her strangely.

Lindsay stared blankly at him. She blinked and the images were gone. *Outhouse? Poodle cut?* Where on earth had that come from?

Her mother had chided her for an overactive imagination, so that must have been what it was. Or maybe a story she'd read.

"You okay?" Eric asked. "I could've sworn you left me for a minute. Reminded me of what Aunt Berina used to do."

"Well, whatever it was, it's gone now."

"Want to take a ride in our new boat?" he asked. "We have to try it out, you know."

"Eric," she said hesitantly, "we need to talk about last night. Are you having a potency problem? Is that why—"

He jumped up from the chair. "I don't want to talk about it."

"But honey, if you are, I understand. Especially with everything that's happened lately. I love you no matter what, and together, we—"

Eric's cell phone interrupted her.

"It's Mark. I have to take it." He bolted out of the kitchen.

Damn. The call couldn't have come at a worst time. They needed to work out their problems, not push them away as if they didn't exist. But from the closed expression on Eric's face, she knew he still wouldn't talk.

She didn't know if impotence was his problem at all; he was much too young. It had occurred to her as a possible explanation, but she shouldn't have blurted it out like she did. From everything she'd ever heard or read, men were extremely sensitive about their perceived masculinity, and when there were problems, they reacted in different ways. All she knew to do was to let him know she loved him no matter what, to support him, and listen when he felt ready to talk.

Okay, she reasoned, that would explain his withdrawal from her, but what about her lack of response to him?

She wandered to the front of the house. Eric was on the porch talking on the phone, so she drifted to the old Victrola.

Would it still work?

She raised the lid of the polished mahogany cabinet. Brunswick, the scripted gold label said on the inside. The top compartment held a turntable and a heavy metallic arm, its rounded end still holding a needle. A slim crank-handle protruded from the outside of the cabinet and the bottom front pulled opened to reveal slots holding old records, some 33 RPMs and a few 78s, each neatly cased in white paper sleeves, all in pristine condition. She thumbed through and discovered a treasury of recordings including classics by Billie Holiday, Irving Berlin's "Lady of the Evening," Enrico Caruso, and even a couple of Gene Autry's records. Probably for Eric, she thought fondly, wondering what he'd been like as a boy.

She picked "Only You" by The Platters and placed it on the turntable. She didn't think it would actually work, but she cranked the handle anyway. When the turntable began to spin, she was thrilled. She placed the arm over the record, and when she heard the first scratching sounds from the cabinet speaker, she felt as excited as if she'd discovered a lost diamond mine.

Elated, and with arms outstretched, she began to dance around the room in big, slow circles.

Suddenly, the lights winked on and off. The music stopped. She halted and, heart sinking, stared at the Victrola. Was it a short circuit?

Before she could check, the lights clicked back on and the machine whirled to life again.

She closed her eyes and, humming along with the music, began her dance again.

The air thickened, and when whispers of the familiar fragrance wafted to her, she felt joyous. Large male hands gently led her in big open circles.

How she loved waltzing with him.

She opened her eyes, but as soon as she did, his touch faded and she was alone in the parlor.

"Eric?" She glanced around the room.

He opened the front door. "Sorry about that. It couldn't be helped. Ready to go?"

He couldn't have been outside; he had danced with her. She had *felt* him.

"Weren't you just here? Dancing with me?"

"I just got off the phone. Let's go."

She stared at him as if searching for an explanation.

"Lindsay, not now. Let's just enjoy the day." Obviously he thought she wanted to talk again, and just as obviously, he didn't.

But that wasn't why she was quiet. If she hadn't seen Eric come in from outside, she wouldn't have believed he hadn't been dancing with her. After an uneasy glance around the room, she ran out the door.

Eric followed her out. On the beach, he took her hand and helped her into the boat.

"Honey, you're trembling. What's wrong?"

"Nothing, really." She stared at the house. What was it about the house that was causing her imagination to soar?

She thought about the stories she'd told when she was very young, stories about another time and another life, of a lover and tragedy, but as she grew older and people began reacting to her stories with ridicule and scorn, the fantasies stopped and faded into memories. In time, even the memories disappeared.

What was bringing them to life now? She didn't need the old fantasies to return, couldn't bear the derision on Eric's face. Especially not now, not when they were having personal problems.

He pushed the boat off the beach, jumped in, and they drifted until he yanked the cord for the motor. When it buzzed to life, he putt-putted them to the middle of the lake. It was nice, Lindsay thought, like gliding over water, but when he cranked it up and they took off, she forgot everything except the thrill of the ride.

Sitting in the front of the small boat, she rode close to the surface and loved the splashing sound the bow made cutting through the water, loved the wind on her face and even loved the earthy, fishy smell of the lake. Never before had she experienced anything so exhilarating. She lifted her face to the sky and felt such peace and happiness in her heart that she wanted to shout with the joy of it.

"Can we go faster?"

Eric laughed. "I don't want to open her up yet. It's better to take it a little slower to see how she handles."

Serpent Lake teamed with life. They cruised by patches of tiny flying insects swarming in circles, and they witnessed a fish jump to snatch one of the bugs out of the air. Seagulls cried above them and crows cawed next to the treed shore.

"Oh look!" she cried, pointing to a large bluish-colored bird about three feet tall perched on a half-submerged log near the bank. Its long slim neck was curved like an 's' and its wings were a bluish-gray.

"A blue heron," Eric said. "Feeds on fish and frogs."

As they approached, the bird took flight and its wingspan appeared six feet wide. Lindsay watched it glide over the far shore and thought again how different this part of the country was from where she grew up. She wondered if she'd ever get tired of exploring, of her delight in discovering something new.

They passed boats of all sizes, ranging from the smaller fishing ones like they had to the larger cruisers. Exploring the length of Serpent Lake, Lindsay couldn't get over the pristine beauty that surrounded her, the lush greenery of the untamed forest bordering sections of the water, the puffy white clouds set against the deepest blue sky.

Farther down the lake, some of the newer log homes as well as older frame houses nestled between trees, some with a sandy beach, others with lawns that simply ended at the water. Lindsay noted boats of various sizes anchored to private docks and felt in awe over life around the lake, how certain things had changed—the newer log and glass homes, larger and sleeker trucks pulling boats, yet other things had stayed the same—the wildlife, the sun's rays glistening on the water, the sadness and nostalgia for something she couldn't name.

Chapter Ten

Back at the house, the first thing she noticed was that spicy scent lingering just under the furniture polish. It wasn't as strong as her first time in the house or even the night before, but it was there, so familiar yet so elusive. It was almost as if it welcomed her home.

"What *is* that smell?" Sniffing the air, she wandered from the foyer and into the kitchen.

"What smell?" Eric trailed her.

"You don't notice anything?"

He shrugged and opened the refrigerator door. "You want to have dinner here?" he asked, pulling out some cheese. "Or do you want to try that fancy place north of Brainerd? One of the guys told me they have great seafood there."

Lindsay was opening cupboards and sniffing inside. "Makes me think of a kitchen spice."

Munching on a chunk of cheddar, he watched her. "What are you doing?"

"Trying to find where that scent is coming from. Did your aunt have a garden? Perhaps I'm smelling traces of that."

"Most people had them, but I doubt anything's still there, though. It's been too long."

Lindsay straightened and sniffed the air. "Oh well. It's gone again."

Later that afternoon the mortuary called and said the cremains were ready. They decided to go ahead and pick them up instead of waiting.

After sunset, Eric carried the octagon oak urn to the beach and Lindsay carefully stepped directly behind him. Although the porch light and the high round moon helped to illuminate their way through the blackness, she had never before seen such black nights as she experienced on the lake. Her eyes began to adjust and she could make out Eric's outline next to her.

"Come on," he told her. "Let's find a better spot." He moved to the far end of the property where the sand ended into the brush. Finding a spot on the bend, almost on a point, he stopped.

"Shouldn't I say something? I'm not particularly religious, but I can't just dump her ashes without anything."

"Say whatever's in your heart."

They silently stood looking out over the water and listened as it gently lapped the shore. In the distance the faint buzzing sounds of a boat motor carried over the water.

Eric opened the urn and held it upside down over the water. Just then the moon slipped from behind the clouds to light the water with shimmers of silver.

"Goodbye, Aunt Frida," Eric whispered. "Thank you for sharing your life and showing me that even when my father was taken away, I could still have family and love. May your journey to the heavens be a wonderful one. I wish you love."

Lindsay's eyes misted. "That was beautiful."

Just then his phone rang. Cursing softly, he let it ring.

"Who could that be?" Lindsay asked.

"Mark, probably. Remember it's two hours earlier on the coast."

Although he didn't answer the phone, the mood was broken and they headed back to the house. She heard him sigh before punching in Mark's number. Once again she wished he could get away for good.

That evening while Eric busied himself in his office, Lindsay soaked in the bathtub, luxuriating in the steamy hot lavender-scented water. Her favorite novel and a glass of champagne sat on a tray next to tub. She tried to read a few pages but was too exhausted to concentrate, and the three glasses of the bubbly had left her floating in a soft cloud. She set the book down.

Lying back, she rested her head on the rim and closed her eyes, dreaming about relaxing summer evenings of roasting hot dogs and marshmallows over a campfire when the children and grandchildren visited, of fishing and boating, perhaps even skinny-dipping with Eric in front of the house when they were alone. As she drifted into sleep, she dreamed of making love in the gazebo under the full moon, just like they'd done …

The air in the bathroom changed, became heavy and faintly crackling as if charged with electrical tension. The light flicked off and a faint spicy aroma grew until it filled the room. In her drowsy state Lindsay breathed in the familiar scent of her lover and smiled a welcome.

The bath water gently splashed and two faint thuds sounded, then she felt the slight touch of lips on hers. Strong arms went around her and pulled her to a muscular body. She felt his smooth skin against her breast and her nipples hardened. The kiss deepened and a tongue slid into her mouth and in the twilight of sleep and awareness, she greeted it with her own. He laid her gently against the back of the tub and nuzzled her neck, just below her ear, and sent shivers to her toes. When he took a nipple into his mouth, she sighed and her legs fell open.

Still drifting between sleep and awakening, Lindsay ran her hands over his broad shoulders and down his body to his erection.

"Let's go to bed where we have more room," she murmured.

He didn't answer. Instead, he kissed her, sucking her bottom lip into his warm mouth and placed her legs around his lean hips. Desperately wanting him, she ran her palms around his neck and down his chest, luxuriating in his smooth skin ... *smooth skin?* She stiffened and made a small sound.

Eric had chest hair.

The touches stopped. Her eyes opened and she was fully awake.

"Eric?"

No one answered.

Blinking, Lindsay peered into the semi-darkness and didn't see her husband, didn't see anyone in the bathtub with her. She could see right through where Eric should have been to the tiles on the bathroom wall.

But that was impossible. He hadn't had time to get out. Besides, she would have heard him or heard the water splash or the door opening. As if not trusting her own eyes, she groped for him, feeling the air all around her, but there was nothing.

If it hadn't been Eric kissing and touching her, then who had been in the tub with her?

Chapter Eleven

Lindsay screamed and scrambled out of the water. Footsteps pounded in the outside hall and the door flew open.

"Honey, what's wrong? Are you all right?" Eric held her wet body close and grabbed a towel.

Weeping, she held onto him. "Don't let go," she begged, frantically looking around the bathroom. "Please don't let go."

He gave her a quick inspection. "I don't see anything wrong, no blood, so you didn't cut yourself. Did you fall?"

Crying, she shook her head. "There was a man …"

"A man where? Let's get you dried off." He ran the towel briskly over her.

"In the water with me …"

Eric stopped drying her. "In the water with you? Just now?"

Sobbing, Lindsay nodded. "He disappeared."

"Honey, no one's here. I would have heard someone come up the stairs."

"But Eric, I *felt* him." Her face flamed. "I thought it was you."

One arm still around her, he grabbed her robe and put it on her as if she were a child, then led her out of the bathroom.

"Look, honey, see my office door? It's open. Not only would I have heard someone come in, but I would've seen him as well."

Lindsay checked his open office door and even sat at his desk. He was right. If anyone had entered the house, especially the bathroom, Eric would have seen him.

But who had been making love to her? Surely it wasn't her imagination; she could still feel his touch.

In their bedroom, he helped her under the covers and sat down beside her.

"Now tell me everything."

She began from when she set her book down and told him everything except the intimate details of the lovemaking. It *was* lovemaking, she realized, remembering the gentle touch that made her feel more alive than she could ever remember. Whoever he was, he hadn't wanted to hurt her, she was sure of that. Instead, he was offering pleasure.

Pleasure? He? He who? That was crazy. No one had been there. She shivered and pulled the covers to her chin.

"And when I opened my eyes—"

"When you opened your eyes," Eric repeated. "That's the key. You'd had several glasses of champagne, and since you don't drink much—"

"I only had two glasses, Eric. I hadn't even touched the third one yet, so I was not tipsy."

"Okay, you must've fallen asleep and been dreaming. Couple that with the champagne. That's the only logical explanation."

"Not everything was a dream! I woke up when he, when—" she broke off. She didn't want to tell Eric she'd felt an erection.

"Think back, honey. You said you tried to read but put the book down, and you lay back and closed your eyes. You even said you dozed."

"Search the house, Eric, please. Search everywhere. Just to make me feel better."

She listened closely while he checked every bedroom and even the bathroom once more before going downstairs. She heard him open and shut the front door, then she heard nothing more until he yelled from downstairs that everything was locked up for the night. When the sound of footsteps ascended the stairs, she tensed.

"Eric? Is that you?"

"It's okay, honey." He walked around the landing to their bedroom. "Nothing there."

"Did you check the attic?"

"There's no one here, Lindsay. I assure you."

"Please, just for me."

He sighed. "All right. Then I'm coming to bed."

In a short time he was back in the bedroom peeling off his clothes. "I don't know what it is about the attic, but I just don't like it up there."

"Maybe it's because the lighting's different. Or it could be the sloping roof." She held the covers for him, and after he undressed, he climbed in beside her.

"Honey, I'm beat." After giving her a quick kiss he wrapped his arms around her and was soon snoring softly.

She cuddled into him, secure in the safety of his arms, but she couldn't close her eyes, couldn't think of anything but what had happened in the bathtub.

The amber numbers of her bedside clock read one in the morning, then two.

Was it actually possible she'd been dreaming? Could something that had felt so real been a dream?

Since no one had been in the house, it had to have been a dream, although she didn't fully believe it. She had felt him, felt his lips on her breast, had felt his erection—and she'd wanted him with a passion she had never known.

My God, what was wrong with her?

Was she so sex-starved that she'd invented a phantom lover?

She and Eric hadn't made love in months. Yet, while she was curious about his decline in interest, she had to admit her desire for him had faded as well. She still loved him dearly, and she believed he loved her, so what was the problem? What had caused both of them to lose their desire for each other?

She'd felt exquisite desire in the attic that first evening, and then again tonight in the bathtub, desire so intense she nearly climaxed, something she didn't experience with Eric.

But no one was there—at least anyone she could see.

What was going on? Something was. It couldn't all be her imagination.

It had to be something about this house.

Starting tomorrow, she'd find out everything she could about the history of the Peterson home.

Finally at daybreak, when the birds started their morning chirping outside her window and the dawn brightened their bedroom enough so she could see that no one was in the room with them, she closed her eyes and fell asleep.

Chapter Twelve

When Lindsay opened her swollen eyes, her stomach was rumbling. She pushed off the lavender coverlet to rise, but discovered her legs were too weak to stand.

Was she coming down with something?

She lay back and burrowed under the covers.

From outside her window, she could hear the birds singing, and in the distance a motorboat buzzed.

She loved this room with the pastel wallpaper, the faded purple posies and green leaves against the crème background. Even though it was faded and peeling in places, she loved the pattern. She remembered pouring over patterns with Mama to select just the right one.

"You don't want the flowers too big," Mama had said, tendrils of her graying-blond hair escaping from her chignon, "or you'll get tired of it too quickly."

"Just as long as it has lots of lavender," she'd answered.

She admired the plaster medallion surrounding the ceiling light fixture, pleased that it was still in one piece and not all chipped like in some homes that had been neglected. She used to pretend to see patterns in the swirls, and even as a child, drew what she'd imagined. What wonderful features these old houses had, she thought now, extras that were full of charm that most new homes couldn't duplicate.

Eric had wanted the larger master bedroom but she'd felt more at ease in the smaller room with the purple posies. She would have liked the bigger bedroom; after all, it looked out onto the lake and should have been preferred. But to her, it would always be Mama and Papa's room. Perhaps if she and Eric redid it, stripped off that awful old mauve wallpaper and bought new furniture, she'd feel more at ease in there.

She glanced at the digital clock. Nearly one in the afternoon. Good Lord! She'd never slept that late in her entire life. Feeling decadent, she stood, but her wobbly legs forced her back on the bed.

Must be the flu.

Picking out patterns with Mama? Staring at the ceiling medallion as a child?

My God, was she going insane?

She'd always been chided for her stories of a long-ago time. Was her subconscious bringing those stories to life?

She thought about last night. Had it all been a dream as Eric said? Or more of her imagination?

But why bring the old stories to life now? She'd successfully repressed them for years, so what was causing them to resurface now?

She'd research the history of the house just as she resolved to do last night. Maybe there was some connection, something Eric had told her about the house that stirred up the old stories. Or perhaps it was something she'd read.

There had to be logical explanation.

Otherwise she was lost.

Still, sitting on the edge of the bed, she hesitated, dreading entering the bathroom.

Well that was just great. Now what was she going to do? Revert back to using the old outhouse in back of the house?

When the pressure of her bladder urged her on, she felt for her slippers, grabbed her robe, and zipped it up to her chin. She wasn't going to face anything unknown in just her gown.

She crept across the landing to the bathroom, paused at the stairs leading to the attic, and looked up, breathing in the air, searching, yet desperately hoping she wouldn't detect that certain spicy scent.

Please let it all be nothing but her imagination.

After a few deep breaths, she detected nothing but fresh air from the open window, so she continued on to the bathroom.

Outside the closed door, she braced herself and pushed open the door—to a sparkling clean bathroom. Eric had scrubbed everything, and all she could smell was the lavender from her favorite scented soaps. What a sweetheart!

Fifteen minutes later, feeling slightly stronger, she dressed in lightweight cotton slacks, and, holding onto the banister, took the stairs to the kitchen.

She wanted to grab a quick sandwich and get to the library. Should she tell Eric why she wanted to research the house? She wasn't sure how he'd feel, especially when she didn't want to tell him why it was so important.

He stood cracking eggs into an iron skillet, and when she heard them sizzle in the hot bacon grease, she realized she was hungry.

"Decide to join the living?" He turned the eggs with a spatula. "I heard you upstairs and thought I'd surprise you with breakfast."

It was such a sweet thing for him to do that she couldn't help but be pleased. Wrapping her arms around his waist, she reached up to give him a light kiss. "Eggs and bacon will do it every time. You just now having breakfast?"

"I had some cereal earlier but thought I'd make my special BLT with fried eggs. Got enough for two if you're hungry."

"Starved." Leaving the security of his arms, she turned to rummage through the grocery sacks for paper plates and napkins when she noticed the dish drainer, coffee pot, and toaster from their California home standing on the counter. Looking around the kitchen, she realized all the moving boxes were gone. "You unpacked the kitchen?"

"Open the cupboards and see." While he said it in a nonchalant way, pride filled his voice.

She opened the cupboards and everything, including the silverware and pots and pans, was neatly put away.

"Oh, honey, how wonderful!"

"Look in the pantry."

She opened the door to rows of canned soups, vegetables and packages of dry goods, all put away on the shelves as if they'd always been there.

"You've certainly been busy this morning."

Shrugging, he slid the eggs onto a platter alongside strips of bacon. "Self-preservation, you know. With a wife who sleeps all day—"

She grabbed a dishtowel and snapped him on the rear. When he yelped, she smiled. Then her earlier fatigue caught up with her and her knees went wobbly. She slid down on the closest chair.

Rubbing his backside, he turned to her. "Hey, not fair. I was going to return the favor, but you look pale. Aren't you feeling well?"

"I don't feel ill, just extremely tired. Must be some kind of bug."

Eric prepared a plate for her and joined her at the table. "Might as well spend the rest of the day resting. Nothing's so urgent you have to get it done now."

"So much I want to do," she said, wiping a glob of runny yoke from her chin. "Since you've done the kitchen, I'm not sure whether I want to get our bedroom unpacked or do the living room next. And the reading nook. It's such a perfect place to relax and read. Then, of course, there's my studio." Feeling somewhat stronger after her breakfast, she sipped her coffee and looked through the window to the blue sky and sunshine.

Such a perfect summer day. The maple and oak branches swayed gently in the breeze from the lake and the sound of motorboats and sea-doos echoed across the water. Birds sang.

"Just listen. I love to listen to the birds. That's what I missed most. I don't know if I'll ever have the radio on again."

He paused in mid-bite. "You missed the birds? When? We had birds at home."

"I said that? Guess I meant … oh, I don't know. It's not important. Honey, feel. No humidity. Let's shop in town for some bookcases and perhaps an area rug for the attic. We can top it off with dinner at one of the local resorts."

"Can't, sorry. I'm expecting a call from Mark."

"He can reach you on your cell."

"We're going over spreadsheets, so I have to be at the computer. You and I can explore later."

"Oh." Disappointed, Lindsay picked up their plates. At the sink she slipped off her gold watch and set it in the windowsill before running hot sudsy water.

She had hoped that spending the summer away from the frantic pace of southern California would allow Eric to relax so they could spend more time together. Finding him after so many years spent alone still felt like a miracle and she wanted to nurture their relationship, attend to it and watch it grow rather than have it wither from neglect.

Fiercely scrubbing the skillet, she was determined she wouldn't live like she'd done before, losing the one she loved, the years drifting by with each day getting worse, sorrow permeating every facet of her life until nothing could get through the haze of grief and pain, drifting in—

"Honey," Eric said, interrupting her thoughts.

Lindsay blinked. *Haze of grief and pain?* What had she been thinking? She hadn't lived that kind of life. Of course it had been difficult when her first marriage broke up, but it hadn't been crippling. They both realized after three years that they were too young. And to be fair, she hadn't loved him like she loved Eric. Her first husband had been more of an escape from an insecure childhood than someone she loved. She'd found stability with Eric, but since he'd had to travel so much, she still spent much of her time alone.

At least she had her art to occupy her time. But now, with fears about her sanity, she wondered if she would be able to paint again.

"Tell you what." Eric came up behind her. "I'll measure for the bookcases you need and if Mark hasn't called by then, we'll go into town and shop around. We might stop for pie at Bertha's, but no dinner out. I need to get back home."

"You got a deal!" Thank God Eric was there to steady her, to keep her firmly in the present. She turned around and wrapped her arms around him, loving him with all her heart.

He accepted the embrace for a moment, then broke away. "You mentioned an area rug for the attic. Why would you want one up there? Won't you get paint all over it?"

His withdrawal stung, but she decided to not let it spoil their day. She turned so he wouldn't see the hurt and finished the dishes. "Since I'll have the entire space to myself, I thought I'd have a sitting area for when I wanted a break but didn't want to lose the mood and come downstairs. I thought I'd have a rug and a couple of chairs, maybe even a small table for drinks or a snack. What do you think?"

"You'll have plenty of room up there to do anything you want, and since I'm going to be busy in my office, you'll also have complete privacy." He eyed his watch. "You show me exactly where you want the bookcases, then relax while I measure."

After resting an hour and downing more coffee, Lindsay stood in front of the bathroom mirror. She ran a comb through her hair and applied lipstick, and after smoothing lotion onto her hands, she reached for her watch in the blue dish. It wasn't there. That was odd. She always placed it in the dish when washing her hands or while taking a bath or shower. Now where could it be? Although she never put it in a drawer, she pulled out the three vanity drawers just to make sure, but it wasn't there. The watch was special to her, the last thing her mother bought for her before she died. They'd picked it out together, both admiring the rose gold bracelet and pink dial. She'd had it almost ten years and couldn't bear to lose it now.

In the bedroom, the first thing she saw was her watch. Right in the middle of bed. Suddenly she remembered taking it off at the kitchen sink and placing it on the window sill. Eric must have brought it up for her. Sliding it on her wrist and grabbing her handbag, she vowed to be more careful.

A few moments later, they walked the tree-lined dirt road until they came to the pavement fronting the modern homes lining Serpent Lake. Some houses fronted the road, but most sat further back on the property and faced the lake. Lindsay loved the glimpses of the blue water between the houses. She felt as if she were on a perpetual vacation.

"Thanks for bringing up my watch," she told him. "I didn't remember leaving it downstairs."

"Your watch? What are you talking about?"

"Didn't you put my watch on the bed?"

"Honey, I went straight to my office until I could get into the bathroom."

"Oh."

"Which reminds me. We may need to think about a half- or three-quarter bath before the kids visit."

Could she have absentmindedly put her watch on the bed and forgotten? It was possible, but why would she do something so foreign to her routine?

"You mentioned a gazebo," Eric said, nodding toward a small one sitting on one of the home's spacious lawns. "I like that idea, so after I get my office set up, I'll think about building one."

"You honestly don't remember one here? I was sure there was a white one, hexagon-shaped I think, just a few feet from the water."

He shook his head. "I would've remembered. You must be thinking of someplace else."

"Hmm," Lindsay said, thinking about the spot where she thought it once stood, just on the other side of that big maple tree near the beach. "Do you have any old pictures?" she asked.

"Not any more. Whatever I had has disappeared over the years."

It was happening again. She had thought the strong feeling of déjà vu she'd experienced when she first saw the house was because she'd seen some old pictures.

If not, how did she know details about the house?

Chapter Thirteen

When they reached City Hall, a red-roofed brick building next to the shoreline, they cut right instead of strolling further down the road to City Park. Two blocks later, they were downtown.

Main Street was busy, but as they discovered before, it lacked the frantic pace of Southern California.

"Just listen," Eric said. "No horns honking, no screeching sirens. A man can breathe here."

Cars lined the curbs on both sides of the street. As soon as one pulled out, another took its place. There were no parking meters; people just pulled in front or behind other cars. But Lindsay didn't get a feeling of hustle and bustle. People on their way to the drug store, the bank, or one of the many antique stores stopped to talk to each other or wave a greeting to someone else.

Lindsay took a deep breath, determined to shove aside her unease and enjoy the day with her husband. She had so much to be thankful for and she didn't want to revert back to her doom and gloom persona. She'd already wasted too many years living apart from the world.

"Ready for some pie?" Eric asked. "Bertha's is just up the block."

"Always ready for homemade pie."

Although Bertha's Diner wasn't crowded, two men and one woman, each dressed in casual office attire, sat at the counter. They had turned around in their seats and were talking to a young couple with two small children in one of the six booths. The clatter of pots, pans and silverware and the wonderful aroma of good food, all mixed with the friendly chatter, made Lindsay feel this diner would be one of her favorite places. They took a booth up front.

Suddenly, all conversation died.

Lindsay smiled at the people at the counter and they nodded a greeting, yet each one of them turned around. The couple with small children were behind Lindsay so she couldn't see them, but she could feel their silence—except for the children, who chattered on to each other.

"What is it with these people?" Lindsay asked Eric. "Do we look like aliens or something?"

Eric, busy glancing over the paper menu, didn't look up. "I'm sure it's nothing to do with us. What are you going to have?"

Lindsay took another glance around the room, thinking of Shirley's reaction that first day, the old woman, and some other strange looks they'd received since arriving. She'd always heard that small towns were friendly, so what was it about them that the locals didn't like?

By the time a server, a heavy woman of about fifty with short kinky hair approached their booth with water, Lindsay was nearly in tears.

"Just in time for the buffet," the woman said. "Hope you're hungry."

Lindsay swallowed. "We're here for the pie, although I'm not sure we should stay. For some reason, we may chase off your customers."

"Oh, some people need a refresher on manners," the server said in a voice loud enough for everyone to hear. She smiled. "You the new folks at the Peterson place?"

"I'm Eric Peterson. My grandparents build that house," he said.

"I know. I'm Bertha and this is my place. Seems I remember something about you moving to California when we were kids. Actually, we went to elementary school together."

"We did? Sorry, I don't remember."

"You wouldn't. I wasn't in your league. Besides, I was a couple of grades ahead. Welcome back. It'll be nice to have the house occupied with people again."

"*With people?*" Lindsay asked. "What does that mean?"

Bertha flushed. "Nothing."

"Please, I need to know."

Eric gave Lindsay a questioning look, but she ignored it.

"Oh, you know how rumors start in a small town," Bertha hedged. "Hobos tend to camp out in vacant homes and it starts all kinds of talk."

"Like what?"

A young male voice yelled from the kitchen for her. She yelled back, "Be right there! That's my grandson," she told Eric and Lindsay. "I'm breaking him in to the restaurant business. I'd better see what's the problem." Bertha nearly ran in her haste to get to the kitchen.

"What was that all about?" Eric asked.

"Oh, just wondering what people think about the house."

Bertha returned to their table carrying two plates of thick slices of pie, each mounded high with whipped cream.

"Juneberry pie," she told them, placing them on the table. "Try it."

Lindsay forked aside some of the whipped cream and crust to reveal a purplish filling, similar, she thought, to a cherry pie, only slightly smaller berries. The first bite reminded her of grape with a touch of cherry and almond. It was wonderful. And slightly familiar.

"I've had this before."

"Really?" Eric asked. "I didn't think you'd been out of Southern California."

"They prefer more of a wetlands to thrive," Bertha said, "although I suppose nowadays the nurseries grow them. Glad you like it."

Lindsay took another taste. How *did* she know that flavor?

"The grandkids pick them and I freeze them for pies," Bertha told them, "that is, when I have any left after making wine. You'll have to try some."

"Can't wait." Lindsay found herself warming to the woman and hoped she'd get a chance to talk to her alone. Bertha knew something about the house, something she didn't want to talk about.

"Once you folks get settled, you should stop by the Woodtick Inn in Cuyuna for the wood tick races. Lots of good fun and some darn good fishing in the area."

Lindsay gaped at her. "Wood tick races? You're joking, right?"

"No joke. They're a big deal around here."

"People actually handle those horrid little insects that suck your blood? And everyone thinks we're strange."

Bertha laughed.

On the porch glider after dinner at home that evening, Eric talked about adding a new bathroom. Lindsay nodded vaguely, thinking about going to the library the next day, hoping to find something to explain what had been happening in the house. And if she went alone, she'd stop at Bertha's. She knew something, and maybe without Eric with her, the woman would open up about the rumors.

"I think I'll go to the library tomorrow and see if they have any information on the house."

"Great idea," Eric said. "They might even have some old photos. Take your time and enjoy yourself, maybe stop in for another piece of pie. And bring some home for me. Bet Bertha will introduce you to some local women and get you into the social life there."

"Not sure I'll have the time for much of a social life, at least not right away. Julia's been after me to get some paintings together for a showing, and I promised her I'd get some together after I got settled."

"Maybe Crosby has an art gallery that would show some of your paintings. That's something else you could check."

"Good idea, although Julia's been so nice that I'd hate to show someplace else."

Eric's cell phone jangled. "That's Mark. Don't wait up." He headed for the front door.

Lindsay hesitated, reluctant to go inside. What if she smelled that scent again?

She spent the next hour watching the moon rise over the lake, listening to the soothing night sounds, but eventually, fatigue won and she headed for bed.

Tomorrow, she hoped, she'd find some answers.

***

After an uneventful night, her first stop the next morning was at Bertha's, but she was told the owner had taken the day off. Disappointed, Lindsay resolved to check later in the week.

As before, people were walking the sidewalks, and when she passed a diner on Main Street, the sound of laughter carried through the open door.

She stopped at the small drug store, and while admiring the Precious Moments Collectibles, a tall glass bottle with a purple label on the toiletries aisle caught her eye. Lavender bath salts. It was more than she normally paid, but feeling as if she'd found a lost treasure, she grabbed the last jar and, along with a spiral notebook, made her purchase.

Outside, she crossed the street to the city block housing the library. Tall pines shaded the modern single-story building and several park benches offered pedestrians a place to stop and rest.

She hoped she'd be lucky enough to find photos of the house and gazebo so she could show Eric. Surely they would have some record of the Peterson house, even if it was over eighty years old. But as she approached the front door, she hesitated, suddenly aware of an uncomfortable knot in her stomach.

What if she did find proof of the gazebo? How could she explain it, even to herself, especially since Eric didn't even remember one? In her mind she could see it, a small white structure, hexagon-shaped, with a pointed top like a spiral. It stood near the water and she used to sit on one of the padded cushions with ...

"Oh, God," she whispered, cutting across the lawn to one of the benches. *Padded cushions?* What was wrong with her? What were these sudden thoughts of a past she never had? Was she truly going crazy?

Chapter Fourteen

Then she remembered a magazine article she'd read on the trip back to California about a young man who developed a brain tumor. One of the symptoms was phantom smells and hallucinations.

Oh, Jesus, she couldn't have something horrible like a tumor, not now. Not when she was finally able to live the life she'd always dreamed of with her husband by her side and a house that felt like a real home.

But that would explain why she could smell the scent when Eric, even when in the same room, could not.

And feel things that weren't there.

A *brain tumor?* Some of them were inoperable. That would mean she could soon die.

No! Not now, she wasn't ready. She had to make Eric love her again, had to fix up the old house, had to see her son again. She couldn't die now. She had to …? She broke out in a cold sweat. Nausea doubled her over.

"Young lady, are you all right?"

Embarrassed, Lindsay looked up. A man in his late seventies was standing in front of her, his loose trousers held up by suspenders, a look of concern on his weathered face. He grasped a cane in his right hand. She tried to smile.

"I'm okay, thanks. Just taking a moment while exploring the town."

"Well, Larry's diner is on the next block if you need something to drink. I don't have a car or I'd take you, but I'll walk with you. Turned in my car and license on my seventy-ninth birthday, you see, but I get around." He held up his cane.

What a sweet man. Lindsay was touched by his concern. Even though his body caved in from age, he had a head full of silvery white hair and a twinkle in his eyes. She bet he'd been quite the ladies man in his time.

"I'll be fine," she told him. "I'm on my way to the library."

"You tell Karen to get you some water," the man said. "Tell her Harry said so. Karen Midthun. I got her that job, you know, thirty years ago. She was just a kid, but she was smart and wanted to work. My wife and I loved to read and we were on the library board …"

As he droned on, telling her about a past important to no one but himself, Lindsay nodded politely and began to feel better. When he wound up his reminiscing or ran out of breath, she assured him again that she was all right.

"You ever want to talk, you ask for me, Harry. Everyone knows me." Tipping an imaginary hat to her, he shuffled to the next block.

It wasn't until he was out of sight that she realized she should have asked him about the Peterson house and the old lady with the frizzy white hair. She could run after him, but she wasn't sure her shaky legs would hold her.

But she should do something positive, something to make her feel as if she had some control over her fate, so the first thing, she'd make an appointment with a doctor for an examination. She would jot down the unusual things that had been happening and take it in, starting with her first experience in the attic ... no, starting when she first saw the house and felt as if it were familiar. She'd list the conditions, time of day and anything else she could think of.

But what if, by any chance, she found a photo of the house with the gazebo, a gazebo that Eric was convinced had never existed. What would that mean?

It would mean she wasn't crazy or that she probably didn't have a brain tumor. But it would force her to admit that the strange things that had been happening to her were real. She didn't understand them, couldn't even comprehend what was happening, but ever since her first glimpse of that house, her world has been askew. Off center.

One explanation was that her wonderful new home was haunted. A haunting wouldn't explain everything, but she could only face one strange occurrence at a time.

Even thinking it seemed ludicrous, and if the episodes weren't happening to her, she'd laugh at the idea. She had never given any of the popular ghost stories any weight, passing them off as products of an overworked imagination or perhaps a lonely soul hoping for some kind of notoriety.

But how could she laugh off a kiss from someone who wasn't there?

Brain tumor or a ghost?

She felt slightly ridiculous, but she finally acknowledged her suspicions and fears.

If it turned out to be a ghost, what would she do about it?

She wasn't sure she could handle it. And even if the impossible proved to be possible, how did that explain the memories of a past she never had?

Deciding she could only handle one preposterous theory at a time, she rose and headed for the library door.

Everything depended on what she discovered.

Inside, Lindsay found the librarian, Karen Midthun. In her forties, she had short brownish hair and her eyes behind the glasses were friendly. Lindsay asked about local records from the early nineteen-hundreds, about the time she thought the house had been built.

"What records we have will be on microfilm." Karen led Lindsay to the machine in the back corner and explained how to find the right microfilm for the years Lindsay wanted.

"Thank you," Lindsay said. "You're as helpful as Harry said you'd be."

"You know Harry Halvorson?"

"I don't know his last name, but I met an older gentleman with a cane outside, on his way to town. He said he knew just about everyone."

Karen smiled. "That's Harry Halvorson, all right. I babysat for them years ago. Nice gentleman and he's been around since the year one. But be careful. He'll talk your ears off."

A harried aide approached her and mentioned something about pre-school children in the reading program trying to climb a table.

"Excuse me," Karen said, then hurried off to help the aide.

Lindsay started with the oldest microfilm and for the next three hours scrolled through pages from the 1920s, 1930s and 1940s, finding the fashions so interesting that she spent more time on the society pages than she had planned.

As she scrolled through, she witnessed high-necked, long-sleeve blouses and ankle-length skirts give way to lower necklines, bell sleeves, and hemlines rising to mid-calf. In the latter twenties, while the department store advertised exquisite flapper dresses, most of the women in the photographs appeared to dress more conservatively, clinging to longer skirts and covered arms. Lindsay stopped to admire what appeared to be the store's last attempt to sell the free-spirited flapper dress, a slim sheath style with scalloped jet and silver beading at the neck and knee-length hemline. She could just imagine a daring young woman dancing in that dress, all flash and sparkles, then how she'd be lectured on proper behavior by all the nice Lutheran ladies of the town.

Turning several more pages, she came to an ivory satin wedding dress with an empire waist and gathered skirt and train. Her breath caught. She couldn't look away. Her eyes hungrily devoured the bodice and short sleeves made of delicate lace with a silk lining. For an instant, she could feel the softness of silk brushing her skin, so cool, yet so warm to the flesh. She could see herself twirling with happiness, watching to see how the satin train settled around her ankles, wishing it were hers, listening for voices from below to make sure her sister didn't return unexpectedly and catch her wearing it.

Then sadness and grief overwhelmed her, so crushing that she could barely breathe. She wondered if she would survive. Lindsay touched the photo, caressing the gown with her finger.

"Are you all right?" Karen asked, standing next to Lindsay.

Blinking, Lindsay glanced up at the woman, horribly embarrassed by what must have appeared to the librarian as strange behavior.

"Yes, thank you. I was just ... thinking of my grandmother's dress. I saw this one and it reminded me of hers." The lie flowed easily but the librarian seemed to accept it.

When Karen moved briskly to attend to another matter, Lindsay sat back and thought about her reaction to the wedding dress. She had *felt* the silk? And listening to make sure her sister didn't catch her wearing it? What sister? That made no sense at all since she was an only child.

It was happening again, those insane thoughts of another time, another woman. And that was twice in a short amount of time. What was wrong with her? Something was going on, but what?

With trembling hands, she jotted down what had happened, where she'd been and what she'd been doing. She described her feelings and the physical sensations she'd experienced remembering how the silk felt.

But how could she remember something that had never happened?

Chapter Fifteen

After she dated her entry, she rose on unsteady legs to find the ladies' room and to get a drink of water. If she were going insane, she could only hope that it wouldn't happen too quickly. She finally had the home she'd always wanted and a husband she adored. She didn't want to lose it all now.

After bathing her face in cold water, Lindsay felt better. She couldn't let one of those spells distract her from her research. No matter if she were teetering on the edge of insanity or if she had a restless spirit haunting her home, she needed to stick to some plan. Only then could she possibly find a way back to normalcy. With determination, she went back to the machine and her notes, this time bypassing the fashion photos.

She found several references to the Peterson family and about Mr. Peterson founding the town bank, building the house on Serpent Lake, constructing roads leading to Brainerd, the county seat about fifteen miles southwest, but there were no photos and no references to a gazebo.

Disappointed, and not sure why she felt that way, she read the society pages about the sisters, Frida and Berina, and their social schedules, and finally, about Frida Peterson's engagement to a young bank clerk by the name of Galen Halidor.

Surprised, Lindsay sat back in her chair. Eric had mentioned that Frida had been engaged once, but both aunts wound up as spinsters.

Who had called off the wedding? And why? He'd been a clerk, the paper had said, so marriage to the president's daughter would certainly have been to his advantage. And from what she understood of history, bank clerks in those days had to be young men of unquestionable morals, so what had happened?

Curious, Lindsay scrolled through the next issues, and there it was: a brief reference to an unfortunate hunting accident involving young Mr. Halidor. He'd been injured, but after recovering, took a position in Wisconsin.

He abandoned Frida? How terrible for her. No wonder there was such an air of sadness about the place.

But why? Did he blame her for the accident? Had she been involved? But why would Berina go into a decline?

Lindsay scrolled further, but found no other references to either sister except a short notation a few months later that they had been sent to a private school.

Intrigued, Lindsay made notes about the family history and printed out some pages to show Eric. She wondered how she could find out more about the family, why the sisters had been sent away and when they returned. She didn't know why she was so interested, but she sensed a connection between the history of the house and the recent events that had plagued her.

The old lady from the diner! Maybe she could be persuaded to talk. And Harry, she felt, would gladly share what he knew, but the old lady might be a problem. Lindsay sensed she knew the most about the family—and the house. She hadn't seen the woman since that first evening, but she'd stop in the diner and check with Shirley.

First, she needed a break. Stretching her cramped muscles, she realized she was hungry and decided to stroll the town and to get some exercise. She could stop in at Bertha's for the lunch buffet and try to find out what Bertha knew about the family and the house. Then she'd check the diner where Shirley worked. Maybe the old lady would be there, and if not, Shirley might know how to reach her.

Gathering her notes and handbag, she stood. Before leaving, though, she'd check out some books on ghosts. Not that she truly believed it, but it wouldn't hurt to do some reading on the subject.

Just in case.

Surprised by the number of books on ghosts and the occult that occupied two wide rows, Lindsay selected three thick volumes about hauntings in America.

"Find everything you need?" the young blonde clerk asked, taking the books to stamp.

"Actually, I was hoping to find more information on an old house in the area," Lindsay told her. "Is there any other place, a historical society perhaps, that might have old photos?"

"There's the Iron Range Historical Society, but it's only open three days a week. You might check there." The clerk jotted down the address and phone number and gave it to Lindsay. She asked for Lindsay's library card.

"My husband and I are new in town, so I don't have one yet."

"No problem." The clerk handed Lindsay a short form. After she entered the information into the computer, the clerk looked at the books. "You must like ghost stories. If you're interested, we have our own haunted house here in Crosby."

"A haunted house here?" Everything in Lindsay tightened, knowing, yet dreading what the aide would say.

"Right here. The old Peterson house by the lake—"

Lindsay felt as someone had struck her. She grabbed the edge of the counter for support.

"It's in a reference book so I can't let it leave the building, but I'll get it so you can see." The clerk left the counter and returned shortly with a large coffee-table-type book. She thumbed through to a certain page, then turned the book so Lindsay could see. She pointed to a photograph.

"Right here."

Still clinging to the counter, Lindsay managed to glance at the book.

The photo of the house was perfect for a book about hauntings, and if she hadn't been so personally affected, she would have admired the photographer's skill. He'd snapped his picture from the front of the house, capturing the sagging porch, the warped steps, and he'd taken it after the moon had risen above the dilapidated house. He'd faded whatever color there was, so the shadows had an even more eerie effect.

Her poor house ...

The caption read:

> *"The vacant Peterson home on Serpent Lake, Crosby, MN, has been the site of several strange occurrences during the years following the owner's move to an undisclosed nursing home. Crosby Police investigated reports of lights flickering throughout the abandoned house and heavy banging noises that echoed across the lake. Reports of vagrants were investigated when boaters spotted the silhouette of a man outlined in the*

attic window. Nothing was ever found."

Lindsay's throat constricted and her pulse pounded in her ears. She could see the clerk's lips move so she knew she was speaking, but Lindsay could hear nothing.

The clerk looked at Lindsay as if she were waiting for her to say something. "Are you all right? Maybe you'd better sit down." She rushed around the counter to help Lindsay to a chair. Then she paled as she obviously realized. "Lindsay *Peterson*, new account. Oh my gosh, you're … please forgive me, I should've made the connection."

"That's okay. I'm fine now." Grabbing her books, Lindsay dashed out the building and sank down on the bench to catch her breath.

Haunted …

Somehow she knew it, had known it from the first, but she hadn't wanted to face it. She still didn't know if she believed it, yet it would explain the strange things that had been happening at the house and in town. She thought of all the odd looks she and Eric had received.

It was all starting to make sense.

Was it possible? Was their house haunted? If it were true, then her theory about a brain tumor was probably false, so she could be relieved about that. But still. *Haunted.* How could that be possible? And why wasn't there any mention of it in the back newspaper issues?

Her breathing settling down, she picked up one book and thumbed through, pausing on pages with photographs of cemeteries with small round spots floating in the air. Orbs, they explained, balls of light believed to be spirits of the deceased.

She hadn't seen any balls of light in her house, but she had certainly felt the shifting of air. And of course there was the spicy scent. Now that she thought of it, it reminded her of an old-time shaving lotion she'd smelled at an antique store years ago.

Antique store! Crosby was full of them. She wondered if any of them would know of the scent.

She thought of Mathews. Why hadn't he mentioned it? Even if he didn't believe it, he should have told them. How could he expect Eric to make an important decision about ownership if he didn't know all the facts? And while rumors of a haunting may not be factual, it would still be something an heir should know.

She hoped the old woman would be in Shirley's diner today. If not, Lindsay had a feeling the waitress knew the old woman and could help Lindsay get in touch with her.

Just please be working today. Lindsay didn't think she could stand waiting another day.

She stood, and when she felt more steady, she headed for downtown.

She was going to find someone to talk to her and give her some answers.

Chapter Sixteen

She passed Bertha's first, and decided something hot and nourishing would give her some strength before facing Shirley. From the way the waitress had clammed up the first night, Lindsay had a feeling it would be a battle of wills to get her to talk.

She hoped she could handle it.

When she opened the door to Bertha's, she was pleasantly surprised to see the owner, but the woman immediately ducked into the kitchen. Strange, Lindsay thought, and it only got more strange.

Lindsay told the cashier, "When Bertha has a moment, I need to speak with her."

"I'm sorry, she's out for the day and can't be reached."

"But I just saw her."

The cashier, a young woman in her late teens, early twenties, shrugged. Her cheeks reddened, and she looked as if she wanted to run too, but she said nothing more.

In the silence, customers at the counter turned and gazed at Lindsay. She couldn't get out of there quick enough.

Why did everyone in town act so strangely? Eric might have inherited a house that was supposedly haunted, but she still wasn't sure. She needed answers, not the silent treatment from everyone she met.

Wasn't there anyone who could, would, help her?

The diner where Shirley worked was doing a brisk business. The noisy buzz of conversation almost drowned out the country music twanging on the radio. Silverware clanked, and the sound of cups scraping saucers could be heard in the lull between the high-pitched squeals of children and the music.

All the booths and tables were full, so Lindsay stood in the doorway. As usual, heads turned to look at her, then everyone quickly lost interest.

Lindsay didn't mind waiting; it gave her a chance to look for the white-haired woman without being too obvious, but to her disappointment, she wasn't there.

With a sinking heart, Lindsay didn't see Shirley either. She waited a few more moments, hoping the woman would magically appear from the kitchen. But she didn't. Instead, two younger waitresses bustled between the kitchen and tables with plates of food.

Was Shirley off today? If so, maybe someone could tell her where she lived. While that wasn't customary in any business, maybe, since Crosby was a small town, someone would tell her. She simply had to talk to her, had to find out how to reach the old woman.

One waitress, a woman about Shirley's age with an apron over her jeans, approached Lindsay.

"The booths are full, but if you're in a hurry, there's a place at the counter."

"Is Shirley working today?"

"She'll be here—" she glanced at the wall clock— "in about an hour."

Thank God. "I'll be back."

Back on the sidewalk, she glanced up and down Main Street, wondering how to fill the hour. She felt too restless to sit and research more articles, but the green canopies over various businesses drew her attention to the antique stores. Browsing would fill the hour and she could look for that spicy scent.

The first one she entered took up two storefronts, and a smell greeted her, but it wasn't the one she'd hoped for. Instead, she caught an old-building mustiness blending with a modern lemon fragrance. Wooden floorboards creaked when she walked. Eric had told her most of Crosby's downtown buildings were original from when it was a booming iron ore mining town during the nineteen-twenties to the fifties.

An elderly lady dressed in a long skirt and puffed-sleeve blouse was dusting an antique roll top desk in the first aisle. She smiled a welcome. Lindsay felt so grateful she wanted to buy everything.

She strolled the aisles, admiring the rose-colored glass lamps, the mirrored vanity trays, the elaborately carved mahogany dressers. She spotted one with a matching stool covered in red velvet just like Mama's. How she'd loved to sit at that dresser and play in Mama's jewelry and makeup, how Mama would get after her for spilling loose powder over the freshly-starched doilies …

Lindsay blinked. Oh no, it happened again! Again with memories that weren't hers.

She had to get out of there.

She hurried down the isle toward the front of the building, when suddenly … she caught a whiff of that spicy scent, the same as the one in the house.

She stopped.

Her heart beating faster, she checked the glass showcases on her left and right holding men's and women's lotions and perfumes. Finally she was going to find out if that scent was a phantom or if it were real.

On her right, a glass showcase held beautiful glass bottles of women's lotions and perfumes. An indigo blue bottle stood on a starched white doily in the center. Evening in Paris, the label read.

She caught a hint of sandalwood from her left. That showcase held numerous men's toiletries, including razors, shaving cream decanters, and colognes. Now she smelled lime. She stepped to her left and realized, with dismay, all the fragrances were beginning to blend.

Would she be able to isolate that certain one?

Displayed on the top of the case were round pine shave crème soaps, a shaving brush held on a small stand, and several cologne bottles. One by one, she picked up each bottle and sniffed. Nothing was right. Frustration and disappointment nearly made her cry.

"Can I help you?" The same woman stepped behind the showcase. "We have some very nice items for gentlemen."

Lindsay blinked back the tears. "On my way out, I caught a scent of something, not sure what it is."

"Can you describe it for me? We have some with a mint base, citrus, and of course spice fragrances."

"What do you have that's spicy? Maybe I'll recognize it."

The woman pulled out three different bottles, opened them one by one so Lindsay could smell. The first two were close, but not quite close enough. But again, they were all smelling alike.

"I'm smelling everything now." She indicated both showcases and her frustration must have shown.

"It is a bit overwhelming here," the woman agreed. "I've suggested separating the showcases, but so far we haven't had the space. Perhaps you need to give your senses a break. Why don't you have a cup of coffee and perhaps one of our homemade strawberry and rhubarb torts from the deli? After that I'm sure you'll recognize the one you want."

Lindsay was so close to discovering the scent she didn't want to leave the counter, but if she could no longer detect that scent, perhaps she must. Just as she was thanking the woman, she noticed an amber-colored bottle with a green and white label. It seemed familiar.

"May I see that one?" When the woman presented it to her, Lindsay took one small whiff—and the familiar spicy scent surrounded her, filling every nerve in her body, triggering her senses with pleasure until she nearly swooned.

She'd found it.

Bay Rum aftershave.

Lindsay examined the bottle in wonder. She knew that fragrance, knew it as intimately as she knew her own name. The scent wasn't phantom. It was real.

"Real," she told the astounded clerk. This time the tears welled and overflowed.

The woman gave her a puzzled frown.

"Dear, are you all right? Do you need to sit down?"

Lindsay felt like singing. "Just tell me about this aftershave."

The woman recited everything she knew. "From what I understand, sailors back in the sixteenth century weren't able to bathe often, and they found that rubbing bay leaves from the West Indies helped with the odor. Around the same time, or at least I think it's about the same time, someone, slaves, I've heard, discovered how to ferment the molasses from the sugar plantations and make rum. Sailors soaked the bay leaves in the rum, then Islanders added other ingredients like lime, and it became popular." She smiled. "I'm sure the company can tell you more."

"I've never noticed it in stores. Can you still get it?"

"You know, I haven't seen it in this area in, oh, thirty or forty years or more. My father used it occasionally, and so did my grandfather, but I think the men today like the other brands the best."

Her father and grandfather.

"Will that be cash or charge?"

Lindsay hadn't wanted to buy the aftershave; she'd just wanted to find it, but after taking so much of the woman's time, she paid.

Clutching the bag, she headed for Shirley's diner.

Maybe now she would get some answers.

As soon as she opened the door, she spotted Shirley wiping down a back booth, the same booth the old lady had occupied that first night. Lindsay hurried toward it before anyone else could take it. Maybe not the best of manners, but after the rude treatment she and Eric had received, she wasn't sure she cared.

When the waitress straightened and saw the next customer was Lindsay, her smile of greeting faded.

"You."

Chapter Seventeen

Lindsay slid into the booth. "I'd like some lunch and then, when you have a moment, I'd like to talk to you."

With a quick, "I'll get you a menu," Shirley bustled away. She dropped off a menu, filled other diner's coffee cups, joked with some, all the while throwing worried glances back at Lindsay.

Lindsay didn't care. She took her time over homemade soup, then a slice of rhubarb and strawberry pie, and lingered over coffee until the diner emptied out.

"Anything else?" The expression on Shirley's face revealed she'd rather be anywhere but there.

"Some answers."

"Sorry, fresh out." The waitress turned to walk away, but Lindsay touched her arm.

"Please. Some strange things have been happening and I think you know something about it. At least help me find that old lady, the one in here that first night. I know she can help me."

Shirley turned to face Lindsay, and for the first time that day, met her gaze. "What makes you think I know anything?"

"The way you and the two men acted that night after my husband told you who we were. And that old lady said something strange. At first I thought she was just a crazy old woman, but now I think differently, and I think you know who she is. Please, I need to find her."

"Sorry, can't help you." She turned and hurried to the kitchen.

Lindsay stared after her, feeling the same as a child whose ice cream fell out of the cone and splattered on the sidewalk.

What could she do now?

No one seemed to want to talk to her. Then, thinking about the rude stares, the silences, she grabbed her bill and headed for the register. Another waitress took her payment.

"Everything all right?" she asked with barely a glance at Lindsay.

She began the customary reply, then changed her mind. "No," she said in a loud voice. "Everything isn't all right." Conversation stopped and heads turned to look at her.

"I'd always heard that small towns were friendly," Lindsay continued. "They sure didn't mean this one. And to think, my husband grew up here and loved this town. Well, as far as I'm concerned, he can have it." With that, she strode through the door.

Outside, she crossed the street, then, a couple of blocks from the diner, she paused. And realized she was trembling.

More slowly now, she headed for home, in no mood to shop for bookcases or anything else.

From behind, she heard running footsteps heading toward her.

"Wait!" A woman's voice.

Shirley.

"Damn, you walk fast. I ran three blocks." The waitress patted her hair back in place.

"Sorry for the inconvenience." Lindsay was heavy on sarcasm.

"Knock off the attitude, will ya?"

"I have an attitude? That's rich. But this town has made me do a lot of things differently."

Shirley had the grace to blush, but she handed Lindsay the sack with the aftershave. "You left your bag. I peeked inside and saw the bottle."

Lindsay took it. "Thank you." She turned to walk away.

"Wait, dammit!"

Two white-haired ladies passing them on the sidewalk paused at the expletive. Lindsay noticed their slacks. One wore pink polyester pants with an artificial seam sewn down the front, the other, yellow. At least they were colorful.

"Working today, Shirley?" One asked, staring with curiosity at Lindsay.

"Just taking a break," the waitress answered.

"Enjoy your day." With another side glance at Lindsay, they walked on. The street was busy with traffic and a diesel pickup, its engine clattering, pulled into the space in front of Lindsay.

She faced Shirley, but said nothing. She waited.

"Look. You're right," Shirley said. "People talk, and the reception you've gotten is pretty shitty ..."

"And?"

"Jeeze, give me a break. This is hard for me."

Lindsay instantly softened. "What's so hard, Shirley? I don't understand. I don't want to hurt anyone, I just want someone to help me understand what's happening."

Shirley chewed her bottom lip.

"I'm either going crazy," Lindsay said, "or there's something going on at that house. After finding this—" she held up the bag— "I think it's the house. Please, I need help."

"Oh Christ, I guess you do." But she said nothing more. Instead, she sighed and shuffled from one foot to the other.

No matter how she tried not to get her hopes up, Lindsay felt encouraged.

"Do you know that white-haired old lady from the first night? After we left the diner, she came up to us and muttered something horrible about the house."

Shirley didn't reply for the longest moment. "What did she say?"

Lindsay told her, her voice quiet. "I just haven't been able to forget it, and I'd like to ask her what she meant. Do you know where I can find her?"

"You sure that's all you want from her?"

"What else could I want?"

"People ostracized her for years, and I can't let that start again."

"Please, Shirley. Something's going on in that house and I need to know what it is. Please help me."

"Damn," Shirley said again. Then apparently making a decision, she said quietly, "Yeah, I know who she is. She's my grandmother."

"Your grandmother?" Lindsay hadn't expected that. No wonder she was so reluctant.

"I can't do anything today," Shirley said, "but tomorrow I get off at five. If you'd like, we could talk then."

After arranging to meet the next day at five-thirty in the park, Lindsay rushed home to tell Eric. She'd found the aftershave, proof of what had been happening. She just hoped he wouldn't brush it off again.

Chapter Eighteen

As soon as she opened the door, Lindsay heard Eric's voice from his second floor office. Still carrying the lotion, she hurried up the stairs.

His hair was ruffled as if he'd raked his hands through it, and for the first time, his desk was cluttered with papers. His computer screen showed a series of spreadsheets.

"Something's wrong, Mark, either in your figures or mine." His voice sounded harried, strained. "I've gone over the last three month's entries several times and the numbers simply don't match with yours."

She waited silently in the doorway, respecting his work, yet nearly bursting with excitement.

Come on, Eric, get off the phone.

He had to believe her this time. At least be curious enough and open-minded to go with her to meet Shirley. After all, it was his ancestors and house.

He was still talking.

She must have made a sound because he glanced at her and held up his forefinger for her to wait.

She held up the bag to let him know she had something to show him. He nodded vaguely, then turned his attention back to Mark.

More waiting, waiting, waiting. Waiting to get anyone to talk to her, waiting for tomorrow to talk to Shirley, waiting, hoping her own husband would believe her.

She tried to curb her impatience. She went to the bathroom to freshen up, hoping that by the time she finished, Eric would be free.

He wasn't.

She wandered through their bedroom, then downstairs. In the dining room, she stood gazing through the bay window to the forest in back of the house. Trees swayed gently in the breeze from the lake. Butterflies landed on wildflowers in the brush, and circling birds called to each other and landed on branches. Squirrels chased each other up and down the oak trees.

Nature. A beautiful thing.

Slowly, she began to relax, to feel at one with the woods and the creatures that lived there. She opened the window wider and breathed in the warm moist air.

Then the air became heavier, almost as though a blanket of humidity settled on the house, but it wasn't quite the same. She felt warm. Alive. Then a faint sound to her right caught her attention, the same sound she'd heard before, a slight vibration, a low hum. She could almost hear his voice.

"What?"

No physical answer, but she suddenly thought about a tree, *their* tree.

Now she was being ridiculous. No one had a TREE.

But standing at the window, she scanned the forest, looking, searching, then she spotted it again, towering above the other trees. The black ash.

As before, she felt an overwhelming affection for that tree, and this time nothing was stopping her, so she dropped the bag with the shaving lotion on the table and ran out the back door. She raced across the dirt road and into the thicket, dashing past the pines and oaks, not even noticing when brambles scratched her arms. She had to get to her tree.

Finally, she stood before the massive old ash and wanted to hug the crooked trunk. Instead, she slowly circled the circumference, searching, knowing something important was there.

She had to find it.

Finally, slightly above her head she saw it, a carved heart about seven inches high, aged to a faded gray so faint it was barely distinguishable from the trunk, its curves misshapen by time and tree growth.

But it was still there!

She stared, caressing each curve with her eyes, not quite believing it had survived the tragedies of their lives.

With wonderment and delight, she reached up to touch it, then on tiptoes, ran her finger around the heart, feeling the bumpy scores of the knife, longing for the connection once more.

And the initials in the middle. *GH loves* ... then an initial she couldn't quite make out, then a 'P.' It was so bumpy from time and the elements that she couldn't be sure, but it had to be an 'F.' Galen Halidor loves Frida Peterson.

Galen. She could almost see his hands working steadily in the bark, curving here, chipping there. And when his eyes met hers, he smiled, such a warm loving smile ...

Her eyes misted, then the joy turned to sorrow, a grief so constricting she couldn't breathe. Tears sprang and overflowed, but still she didn't lift her fingers from the heart. Just to touch where he had touched, and she almost remembered ...

"Lindsay? What are you doing out here?" Eric's voice broke the enchantment. "Are you crying?"

Flustered, Lindsay dropped her arm and swiped her eyes. "I don't know." She glanced back in confusion at the tree. She didn't know what she was doing or why she was crying. Still, the feeling of intense loss continued.

Insects buzzed around them. A dragonfly darted in front of Lindsay, its transparent wings powerful enough to hold it steady in front of her. After seeming to study her, it dashed off. Souls of the dead, she'd read. Another Native American legend.

Eric slapped a mosquito on his neck.

"Let's get you out of the woods." He put his arm around her shoulders to urge her forward.

She looked back. Couldn't he see the heart? *GH loves Frida.* But how could she have known the heart was there?

"Did you see it?"

He kept walking. "See what?"

"The heart. GH and FP. I'm sure it's Galen and Frida."

He shrugged. "Probably. After all, they were engaged." With that, he dismissed it.

"But Eric, I knew it was there."

"You're getting fanciful again, and I don't have time to discuss it with you." Glancing at her stricken face, he soothed. "I don't know. Maybe you heard someone talking. Listen, I have to call Mark back. Something strange is going on."

"Eric, you need to listen. This is important, as important as your phone call."

They entered the house. Lindsay told him about the shaving lotion and meeting Shirley at the park. She didn't tell him she'd discovered their house was haunted; she knew that would be too much right now. Even so, he made listening noises, but she knew he wasn't paying attention. He retrieved a light beer from the fridge and headed for the stairs.

"Eric, please. Will you go with me to see Shirley?"

As if he were humoring an imaginative child, he stopped. She could almost see his eyes roll.

"What for? I don't need anyone to tell me about my family." He started to climb again.

"You'd better listen. Things have been happening to me, and they're not all my imagination. I wasn't going to tell you like this, but I found proof this house is haunted."

"For God's sake, Lindsay. That's ridiculous, and I don't have time for it right now. Someone's embezzled most of the company's funds, and if I can't come up with a solution, the company will go down. *We'll* go down. Besides," he said, halting to look down at her, "we've been over it before."

"But Eric, if you don't believe me, go to the library. This house is actually in a book about haunted houses."

"I have enough to worry about right now, real things, not the product of someone's imagination."

"It's not my imagination. That smell I've been telling you about? It's real. I found it!" She ran to the dining room for the lotion and showed him the bottle.

"What's that suppose to prove? Maybe Grandpa used it, or maybe one of his friends. Hell, it could even be from one of my aunt's suitors. These old houses hold smells."

"Go with me tomorrow. We'll stop at the library and I'll show you the book, then we'll find out what that old woman knows. After all, you left when you were a child. Don't you want to know?"

"I don't have time for this nonsense. Right now I have to try and save the company—and my job." Without another word, he hustled up the stairs.

Lindsay's cheeks flamed. She stared after him. While he'd kept his voice calm, she couldn't help but feel as if she'd just received a reprimand. This was the first time he'd ever spoken to her in that tone and she had to swallow her anger.

From above, the door closed. Firmly. Dismissing her, as if he were the father and she an irritating child.

His job was important, she always understood that, and right now it must be in a crisis, but wasn't she just as important?

If only he would have said, even placatingly, he had to devote his time to the job right now, but as soon as he could, he'd help her discover what they could about the house, she would have understood. And felt better. Even if he had a rational explanation for everything that had happened, she would have known it was important to him simply because it was important to her.

Obviously it wasn't.

She set the lotion on a hall table and wandered back to the dining room, back to the bay window.

Not only did he not believe her, but he'd scoffed at her, made her feel ridiculous, just like everyone in her past with whom she'd shared her stories. She never imagined he would let her down like that. She thought they were closer, had thought he believed in her honesty and integrity as she believed in his.

But what about his physical withdrawal from her? He hadn't shared that with her, hadn't considered her feelings enough to talk to her about what he was experiencing. They were beginning to live like two roommates, each with his or her individual problems, living their separate lives with no emotional ties to each other.

Oh Eric, what's happened to us? Why can't you have enough faith in me? Why can't you trust that I love you enough to overcome anything?

Outside, the sunshine lit the trees, shrubs, and underbrush with gold, but even that didn't help. Lindsay felt as if something precious had just died.

She stood several more minutes, then from deep inside came a spark of determination. She'd find out everything she could about the family and the house. She'd talk to Shirley and her grandmother tomorrow. And if Eric didn't believe her, that would be okay. She vowed to learn the truth for herself, knowing that even if it wasn't important to anyone else, she needed to know for herself.

Feeling a new strength, she took a deep breath and decided to go back to town, to shop for some bookcases and some lavender body lotion. Or to simply walk around the park, to sit on one of the benches and watch families enjoy the lake.

Just as she gathered her handbag, Eric ran down the stairs.

"Mark needs me in California. I've booked a flight out of Minneapolis, so I'll need you to take me to the

Brainerd airport. If we hurry, I can catch the next shuttle."

Chapter Nineteen

She didn't even stay to watch his plane leave; instead, she dropped him off with a perfunctory kiss. He looked questioningly at her a moment, but she didn't smile.

"Have a good trip," was all she could manage, then she hit the gas.

After her dinner of a hot beef sandwich in Crosby, Lindsay headed home, but once she pulled into the driveway, she felt edgy and wasn't ready to settle in for the night.

She dropped her keys and handbag on the porch swing and walked to the shore.

Finding a small stone, she kicked it toward the water, kicking again and again until it hit the water with a soft plop. She watched the ripples grow and dissolve.

On the way to the airport, Eric had said very little, only that he didn't know how long he'd be gone. He gave her the hotel number where he'd be staying.

How could he have left without acknowledging how upset she was? She knew his work was important, but didn't their marriage deserve equal consideration? Couldn't he have said something about working out everything when he got back? Anything to show he cared?

Maybe she was being selfish. Maybe she had to set aside everything she was going through and be a supportive wife to him. But she thought she had been. What else could she do? Right now she didn't seem to know anything—only that she felt miserable.

And now she had her own problems, problems Eric didn't want to recognize. Or believe.

She searched the sandy beach for pebbles large enough to throw, and after pitching several, she searched again for a couple of rocks. She threw one after the other, finally gaining satisfaction when the last one about the size of her fist hit the water with a loud splash.

Now she could take a deep breath.

She headed for the house but her steps slowed. Something felt wrong. She walked further. The air seemed to swell and undulate like it does when a character in a movie is dreaming.

But she was awake. Dusk had settled and the house stood in shadows, reminding her of the photo in the library.

She stared into the shadows, fully realizing she was going to have to stay in that house alone.

Her steps faltered, but she made it to the porch. She broke out in a sweat. Wasn't vision distortion another sign of a brain tumor? That nagging fear inched its way back into her consciousness and she nearly laughed at her earlier thought. Which would she rather have, a brain tumor or a ghost?

She sat on the swing, wondering what to do.

She didn't know anyone well enough to visit in town and didn't want to head back to Brainerd for a movie. Besides, she knew they were excuses to avoid entering the house alone.

Maybe she wouldn't have to—at least at night. Maybe she could sleep on the porch. It was warm enough. And the night was beautiful enough to enjoy sleeping under the night stars.

The moon was rising above the far shoreline, its glow casting silvery reflections on wispy white clouds below. The gray night sky, the blackened tree-line shore, and the gray water with the sparkling silver reflections appeared magical, and Lindsay wished she were a photographer so she could capture the scene just as it appeared tonight. Maybe tomorrow before meeting Shirley, she would shop for a good camera, an easy one to operate, and she could paint from her photos.

Something sharp dug into her hip. Her keys. Her handbag sat next to them. She shifted again, still reluctant to open the front door and go inside.

This was ridiculous. She couldn't spend all night on the porch. She needed a pillow. A blanket. The bathroom. And was she planning to stay on the porch the entire time Eric was gone?

Damn him! Why hadn't he taken her with him? Even though he didn't believe any of the things she'd told him, he should've known she was experiencing something strange and should have either stayed with her or insisted she go with him.

But he didn't. And now she was sitting alone on the porch, afraid to go inside her own home.

But, she reasoned, if the house were truly haunted, if the ghost was real, he hadn't tried to harm her. Instead, it—he, had shown affection.

Desire.

Still, it was unnerving and she wasn't ready to face what might happen once she was alone.

How much longer could she sit outside?

A breeze rolled in from the water, raising the fine hairs on her arms. She shivered and wanted to go inside.

Would that scent surround her again? Remembering what had happened in the bathtub— and her response, was she fearful of what could happen?

In the rush to get Eric to the airport, she hadn't let herself think about being alone. She felt safe on the porch, which was absurd since the porch was part of the house, but she had never noticed the scent there.

And now, she needed to go inside or sit out there all night and freeze.

Would her phantom lover return?

She had urged Eric to face what was happening. Wasn't it time she did the same? She had to face her fears, face whatever was waiting for her inside that house.

Once in the foyer, she paused and inhaled deeply until the absurdity struck her. She thought of the old bloodhound in *Lady and the Tramp* and laughed. Still, she waited until she was sure she couldn't detect anything unusual.

Feeling foolish, she locked the door, then dropped her keys and handbag on the hall table. After pouring a glass of wine, she took it upstairs to watch her bedroom TV, but felt restless and edgy. She'd love to relax in a tub of hot water, but after what happened last time, she didn't dare risk it. Yet it would feel wonderful, and she'd have the chance to try her new salts.

She gathered her pjs and an old ribbon to tie back her hair, and drew her bath. The scent of lavender filled the air. In her robe, and feeling more ridiculous that she could've ever imagined, she stood and addressed the air.

"I don't know if you're here, I don't even know if you're real, but just in case, I'm asking you, begging you, to please go away. I'm alone in this house and I don't want to be afraid. Please ..."

She waited a few moments, glancing around the room at the ceiling, upper corners, expecting ... what? A disembodied male voice saying he'd go away?

Absurd. The entire thing was beyond belief.

Nevertheless, she waited a few more moments, then slipped out of her robe and into the tub.

An hour later, she crawled into bed and picked up her book, but she soon realized she was automatically turning pages without even knowing what she'd read.

The quiet house was too quiet. She thought of turning on her CD player, but decided she didn't want to get out of her comfortable bed to do it now. She glanced around the room, and not finding anything amiss, she went back to reading. Or turning pages.

A slight noise sounded from below. She listened intently for a few moments, then decided it was probably the refrigerator cycling.

What was Eric doing right now? Was he busy with Mark, or was he also spending a restless night?

She glanced at the clock. Only eleven? With Eric's scheduled stops, his plane had barely touched down in Los Angeles. He hadn't called, so maybe he was using his time alone to think about their marriage, but she wouldn't bet on it. He'd seemed far too preoccupied with business.

If she went to sleep, this endless night would pass more quickly, so she turned off the light and sank into her pillow.

But she couldn't sleep; everything was still. Too still. No crickets, no buzzing horseflies, no frogs with their croaking noises to each other. All the normal night sounds were quiet.

Then she heard it again.

A slight splashing from the lake, a sound like someone hitting the water in a belly-flop.

But no one would be swimming at midnight, would they? And certainly not in front of her property. It could be someone night-fishing. She couldn't sleep until she checked.

She hurried out of bed and rushed to the window. The full moon rode high overhead, casting silver streaks on the inky water below. If she hadn't been on edge, she would have thought it beautiful. Almost magical. The air felt soft, and because it was so still, she caught the fragrant scent of honeysuckle. Someone could be out enjoying the night, but after scanning the water, she didn't see anyone on the lake.

Wispy bands of clouds drifted across the sky, veiling the moon into total darkness. Lindsay heard that strange slapping sound again. Just as the moon emerged in all its splendor, she saw something. She leaned forward, squinting in the darkness.

There, right in front of the property, a circle of bubbles appeared on the water as if a large fish had surfaced, then submerged again.

What could it be? Even the largest walleye ever recorded wasn't capable of making a circle that large. It was almost as if a whale or dolphin had been swimming on the surface. But of course no ocean mammal would be in a north woods lake.

Maybe not a whale or dolphin. Maybe ... even knowing it was nonsensical, she searched the water for lumps, bulges, or anything else she'd heard described about the Loch Ness monster, but clouds hid the moon again, and Serpent Lake became, once again, too dark to see anything. Just in case, she kept watching, scanning the water's blackness for signs of Crosby's famed lake creature. She had to make sure it wasn't there, had to make sure she could sleep safely in that isolated lakefront property.

Finally, after minutes or hours, she turned from the window and padded back to bed.

A noise again. Her eyes popped open. Would this night ever end?

This time she heard a different sound, like a brief sizzle, similar to static electricity when touching someone after walking on carpet. The lights flickered.

Was the electricity shorting out? If so, an old house like hers could catch fire in minutes.

Alarmed, she got out of bed, padded barefoot to the door, and cracked it open. She stood listening; everything seemed okay. The soft night light in the foyer was burning steadily now, and the crickets had resumed their noise.

But there had been something else, some presence. She felt it in the air's heaviness, then she caught the slight scent of Bay Rum. Even that seemed to be fading.

He had been there, and while he had made no move toward her, she hoped whatever it was would stay away—at least until Eric returned. It was too much for her to handle alone.

Sometime later, after two glasses of wine, she lay back in bed and let her heavy eyelids close. The sharp sizzle sounded again, the stairway lights flickered, then her bedside lamp winked on and off, but she barely noticed as she fell deeply into sleep.

Chapter Twenty

He came to her when the moon was high, this time taking the chance of lying beside her sleeping form. This was the woman he loved, the one for whom he'd waited decades to return.

And finally, through some miracle, she was here.

With his head propped on his hand, he reveled in the sight of her, breathing in the familiar scent of lavender, allowing himself the luxury of feeling her warmth next to him. Although he ached to make love to her, to finally complete the love that had been interrupted so long ago, he didn't want to risk frightening her again.

She sighed in her sleep, and he felt an irresistible need to touch her. Maybe if he were careful, she wouldn't wake.

Barely touching, he tenderly traced the curve of her lips, her chin, then caressed the softness with his lips. He took his time, glorying in her body, savoring each touch.

She sighed, her breath fragrant with the fruity aroma of wine, but didn't wake.

Promising himself he would just look, he lowered the sheet covering her, and softly, lightly, unbuttoned the pajama top, filling his gaze with the sight of her.

He couldn't help himself. Her breasts were created to be caressed. Just large enough to fill his hands, he cupped them, watching carefully to see that she didn't wake. When he felt safe, he licked one pink nipple, then the other before taking one into his mouth.

Her breathing changed, and he stilled his movements until she slept soundly again. Ever so gently, he lowered her pajama bottom, exposing the vee of her legs. Fine hair the color of new wheat covered his place of worship. How he wanted her, how he longed to be inside her, to feel every inch of her skin against his, but he wasn't ready to risk frightening her further. She hadn't fully realized who she was, and acknowledging him might be too much for her—yet.

But he could take his pleasure in another way.

He lowered his head and tasted her upper legs, lavishing his attention on the silky skin of each inner thigh.

She moaned and opened her legs.

He moved closer to the vee, the hairs brushing his nose, breathing in the womanly scent of her. With his lips and tongue, he gloried in his beloved, ready to worship her forever.

***

Wave after wave of pleasure filled Lindsay, and, gasping for air, she woke, the sensations so intense she thought she'd die of it. Never before had she felt anything so breathtaking. She turned to her husband, to embrace him, to tell him how wonderful his lovemaking had been, but no one was there. She fully woke and the realization hit her.

Eric was in California.

Someone just made love to her.

Had it been a dream?

But her body was still reacting, still throbbing in the aftermath of the most powerful orgasm she had ever experienced.

Pulling the sheet to her chin, she scooted back against the headboard, watching, guarding.

A strong wind whished through the house, and just below the sounds of branches brushing the house, leaves rustling, she heard something else, a resonance, a whisper floating in the air before fading.

"Remember … remember."

***

The next morning she woke, so listless she could barely get out of bed.

Not bothering with her robe, she staggered downstairs and made coffee, standing by the coffee maker while it dripped. She downed the first cup so fast she burned her tongue, but it was only after her second cup that she could concentrate.

Last night had been a nightmare filled with mythical monsters. Not only a ghost, but also a sea monster. Had she been asleep and dreamed it all? A ghost, if there was truly such a thing, was ethereal, a spirit with no physical body, incapable of making physical love. So it couldn't have been real. Remembering how she'd responded, she decided it must have been the female version of a wet dream.

After her third cup, she still felt heavy fatigue, so she dropped bread into the toaster. Maybe something in her stomach other than caffeine would help.

"Remember," he'd said, as if she should know him. If the lovemaking had been a dream, then his words had been her imagination. If so, why did they linger in her memory? Why did she feel if she could only remember, she would have the key to everything that had been happening?

Remember … remember.

An image formed in her mind, lingered for a heartbeat, then was gone. Her heart quickened, as if recognizing a treasure believed to be lost.

Was it the lover from her dream? She tried to visualize his features, to capture the eyes, but try as hard as she could, his image remained just beyond her perception.

Could she paint him? Not if she couldn't recall how he'd looked. Yet, there had been times in the past when something from within guided her strokes and she created a painting entirely different from what she had intended.

Could that happen again? Would her subconscious allow her to paint a portrait from her heart?

She had to try. Now. Before his image was gone forever.

The toast forgotten, she dashed upstairs to the attic, frantically digging through still-packed boxes of art supplies and spreading them on the floor. Once she had a canvas and her paints ready, she began. One long stroke to outline the face, then … nothing. She didn't even know if the face outline was accurate.

She tried again. Maybe if she held the brush next to the outline, her hand would begin to move, like when trying to contact a spirit with a planchette from an Ouija board.

Still nothing. Maybe she wasn't concentrating hard enough. She tried again, eyes closed, her brows scrunched in a frown.

Was that a face she was seeing? She moved the brush a stroke, then two, then nothing. After a few more determined and unproductive moments, she felt foolish and dropped her arm.

It wasn't going to work. Maybe the image truly wasn't there. Maybe the entire thing was rubbish. Of course it was. There were no such things as ghosts, and if, by the barest possibility they did exist, they certainly didn't make love to the living.

"I truly am ready for the funny farm," she said. "You're not real." She twirled around, crying to the barren attic. "If you are, why are you doing this to me? Who are you? I need some answers! Help me!"

She waited, expecting … what?

Feeling even more ridiculous, she gave up and began to clean her brushes. Maybe it was all was rumors and gossip, and she should see a shrink.

The first hint of Bay Rum was subtle, so delicate she wasn't even aware. She dried the first brush and stood it, bristles up, in a red-splattered jar. Then she noticed the scent. It filled the air and she raised her head, breathing it in. She began to paint.

Three hours later, covered in sweat, Lindsay lowered her brush onto the easel, wiped her hands on the rag, and stood back from the canvas.

She'd captured a face, a young man with Nordic features. Mid-twenties, bluish-hazel eyes with a touch of green that complimented his blond hair and brows. His features were strong, and she sensed he was tall enough to stand well over her five-ten height.

But it was the love—and sadness—in his eyes that tore her heart. She couldn't look away. Her eyes welled and spilled over. The grief was like nothing she'd ever experienced before, and she couldn't stop the tears.

A heartbeat or an eternity later, the scent faded, and just as the last hint waned, Lindsay felt a slight pressure on her lips, a kiss as delicate as butterfly wings.

She gingerly touched her lips, then studied the painting, the questions in a whirl of confusion. Who was he, and what was happening to her in that house?

Maybe Shirley would provide the answers.

She hurried downstairs for her cell phone, took a photo of the painting, and got ready for her meeting in the park.

Chapter Twenty-One

Armed with the photo on her phone, Lindsay arrived at the park about four-forty. Knowing she was early, she strolled past the skating park and found a bench on a little knoll overlooking the water. Behind her in the play area, children shouted from the monkey bars, their mothers watching in the warm sunshine. The dock was busy with cars and RVs pulling up to launch fishing boats. Farther down the shore, people fished from a dock by the city hall.

She watched the activity, checking her watch, wishing Shirley would be as eager as Lindsay to talk. But the waitress didn't appear. At five-twenty, Lindsay scanned the area. Still no Shirley. The park was only a five-minute walk from the diner. Had she changed her mind?

At five-thirty-five, Shirley strolled onto the grass carrying a white paper sack.

"Sorry, but I had another stop to make. I have to get back soon, so I can't stay long."

Oh no, was she sorry she'd agreed to talk and was trying to get out of it? Lindsay had to be careful in her words, had to placate her, anything to keep her from running.

"I appreciate your meeting me at all." She tried to keep the impatience from her voice. "I have so many questions—"

"Before I get into all that, let me feed the ducks. With work and family, I don't get here as much as I want."

Nearly screaming with frustration, Lindsay wondered if she could endure another second. But she doubted the woman would respond as well or be quite as open if she pushed it too hard, so she called on every ounce of patience she had.

Shirley opened the sack and threw crumbs at a small family of ducks swimming close to the reeds.

"I like to feed them. It's calming."

Calming? The ducks raced for the bread, squabbling and diving for crumbs, their quacks attracting others from across the lake. Finally, when the sack was empty, Shirley sat quietly, still not looking at Lindsay.

Lindsay kept her eyes on the ducks too. What was the best way to start the conversation? Should she ask questions about the old woman? She was desperate to discover what the woman knew about the house and family, yet it might be rude to plunge right in.

"Did you know Frida wanted the house burnt to the ground?" she finally said. "It was in the will."

Shirley said nothing and was silent for so long, Lindsay wondered if she had changed her mind and decided not to talk at all.

Finally, "Maybe they should. No one will go near the place, no workman or anyone else."

"Then everyone believes it haunted?"

For the first time since sitting next to her, Shirley faced Lindsay. "How much do you know about it?"

Lindsay wasn't sure if she should mention her encounters with the ghost, spirit, or whatever it was. At least not yet. Better to keep the conversation general—until she felt she could trust the woman.

"I didn't know anything at first, just bits and pieces Eric remembered from his childhood. He spent summers with his aunts until he was about eleven and loved it."

"Why is it so important you talk to my grandmother? What's been happening?"

Heat rushed to Lindsay's face.

"You've seen him." Shirley watched her closely.

"I haven't actually seen anything, but strange things have happened, things I can't explain."

"Such as?"

Lindsay ached to confide in the woman, but she hesitated. Some of it was too bizarre for anyone to believe.

Yet she needed to trust someone, and the woman did say something about *HIM*.

Without revealing the intimate details, she talked about the Bay Rum scent, finding the tree's initials, and sensing someone in her bathroom. She left out the vivid details. Still, Shirley was horrified.

"You need an exorcist instead of my grandmother. Least of all, you have to get out of that house."

"Eric doesn't believe any of it, and he loves it there. I'd think it was all me, but that first night in the diner, you and the others acted so strange. Then your grandmother's warning. I went to the library and found out the house is actually supposed to be haunted." She went silent, gazing at the water, watching boaters cruise by.

"Sometimes," she finally said, her voice so low that Shirley leaned in to hear her, "I just know someone's there. I can't explain it, but I know." She turned to the woman. "I can't believe this is happening. Not to me, not in this day and age. Am I going crazy?"

The waitress studied Lindsay intently, then sighed. "This is hard, you know. Gran tried to warn people for years, but they made fun of her, so we just don't talk about it anymore."

"I'm sorry," Lindsay said. "But please, you've got to help me."

"What did your husband tell you about his aunts?"

"Only that they were good to him and that Frida took care of Berina. She was supposed to have a mental condition, but he didn't see any problems, other than Berina was a bit spacey at times. Of course he was just a child. What are you getting at?"

"Gran thinks the ghost haunts that house because of the sisters."

"Good God why? Who's the ghost supposed to be?"

"Kind of a long story, but I'll try to make it brief."

"Tell me everything, please."

"Gran worked in the Peterson house back in the days when it was in its heyday. People around here still talk about the old Peterson place, and how grand it was. The Petersons were the social elite at that time, you know, him being the bank president and all. They were like royalty for these parts. And the house was the grandest place, all fresh and new." She stared out at the lake. A breeze blew off the water, rustling the leaves on the trees near the bench. She shivered.

"Please go on."

"Well anyway, Gran started working there when she was a teenager, helping Tilly, the general housekeeper and maid. She got lots of overtime at all the social affairs. She liked the two girls. Frida was year or two older than Berina. Berina was adopted, you know, although no one talked about it. Everyone knew, though. When Frida was eighteen, she fell in love and planned to marry a bank teller."

"Galen Halidor."

Shirley turned a questioning glance at Lindsay.

"Read about it in the library."

"Yeah, well, just before they were to be married, Miss Frida shot him."

"In a hunting accident, although I didn't know it was Frida who shot him."

"Wasn't no hunting going on in the parlor at night."

"The parlor? But he was okay. The paper said he left for a position in Wisconsin."

"Oh he left all right. In a box."

"But the paper—"

"You have to understand the Petersons were grand people and had done a lot for the town. Gran said the paper didn't want to cause more harm to that family."

"My God. Poor Frida, to have killed her own fiancée. No wonder the house is so sad." She was silent a moment, then, "Wait a minute. Why did Frida shoot him?"

"No one knows what happened except Frida and Berina, but Tilly testified at the hearing that Mr. and Mrs. Peterson were out of town that night. Miss Frida said she woke to strange noises in the house, thought someone was attacking Miss Berina, so she shot him. It was young Mr. Halidor."

"How terrible—for all of them. Was Frida charged with the shooting?"

"It was filed as accidental, but it changed that family. Miss Berina had a breakdown and Miss Frida took care of her. The whole family kept to themselves."

"I don't understand. If Frida suffered the trauma of shooting her own fiancée, why would she devote her life to her sister? It doesn't make sense."

"We'll never know. It all sort of went away, except for the gossip. Old man Peterson retired, and nothing much was heard from them until they died. Him first, then a year or two later, she passed. Oh, they'd go to church, but still kept to themselves. The girls lived pretty quiet until, oh, sometime in the sixties, when Miss Berina died. Then Miss Frida lived alone until she was sent to the nursing home."

"God. A lot of tragedy for that family."

"The house has been empty ever since. Until you guys came—except for the ghost, of course—if you believe the rumors."

"You think it's the fiancée?"

"Gran thought so. Said Miss Berina used to cry and talk to the air as if someone were there, but why Miss Berina, instead of Miss Frida, would see him is beyond me. But someone or some *thing* was there. For years afterward, even until right before you came, people boating by the place reported a man's outline in the attic window."

Although she should be frightened by the mounting evidence of a ghost in her home, Lindsay felt a surge of excitement. The ghost was real—or as real as a spirit could be, more evidence she wasn't crazy, wasn't hallucinating, and didn't have a brain tumor.

She couldn't wait to tell Eric the story. She was sure he didn't know his aunts' involvement in the shooting and certainly had no idea of the tragedy surrounding it.

She felt validated.

And resentful.

As much as she tried to ignore the feeling, it surfaced like the area's fabled lake serpent, confronting her, refusing to go away.

Why hadn't he believed her? Even if he couldn't support the idea of a ghost, he could've had enough faith in her to be open to possibilities. Anything other than the condescending ridicule he'd shown. She'd endured enough of that in her childhood.

Now she wanted proof of the ghost to show him.

She picked up her cell and clicked through to the photo.

"Do you recognize this?"

Shirley shook her head. "Who is it?"

"I'm hoping the old woman can tell me. Heavens, I can't keep calling her that. What is her name?"

"Elsie, Elsie Hall, but you can't talk to her."

"But she made a point of warning me, so she must be concerned. I was hoping she'd be with you today."

"She won't be talking to anyone for a while. Maybe never again."

"But—"

"She had a stroke after talking to you that day," Shirley interrupted, "and she hasn't regained consciousness. They don't think she'll make it."

After offering condolences, Lindsay headed home, the old woman's fate on her mind. How sad for Elsie. To have been scorned most of her life, then to have it end without knowing she'd been right. Or, without the town knowing there truly was a ghost at the Peterson home.

Was she doomed to the same fate?

Because now Lindsay was convinced it was true. And she felt in her heart it was the fiancée, Galen Halidor. Why he seemed to be haunting her, she had no idea—unless she were connected to his past. Even though such a thing seemed incredible—and impossible, her mounting suspicions were telling her it was true. And if so, was it revenge because Frida had killed him? Yet the episodes weren't frightening. The ghost seemed tender. Loving. Maybe he simply wanted to be near his fiancée. But, she reasoned, if that were so, wouldn't his spirit have left the house once Frida passed on?

So many questions …

Maybe, with more investigation, she could find some answers.

Chapter Twenty-Two

Lindsay wondered how to find Harry. If anyone were old enough to have been around when the tragedies happened, it was Harry. He might be able to fill in some details.

How to find him? Karen—at the library was the best place to start. It was probably closed, but Lindsay felt desperate enough to try.

Sure enough, the doors were locked, the building dark except for a couple of night lights over the counter.

Harry had talked as if he knew everyone in town, so perhaps someone at one of the diners would know him. But how could she find out? She couldn't see herself simply walking in and announcing she was trying to find Harry. So, as anxious as she was to find him now, she had to wait until tomorrow to begin the search.

Before going home, she thought about Mathews. If the entire town knew about the Peterson house, why hadn't he warned them? Surely it was something she and Eric should have known before deciding to keep the place. Certainly before moving in.

What else did he know?

She hurried down Main Street toward his office. She didn't know his hours, but it was well past seven, way past the time most businesses in town closed. But she was hoping to catch him before he left.

When she arrived at the door to the stairs, it was unlocked. His office was dark except for a single lamp on his secretary's desk. Had she missed him? But wait. A sliver of light shone underneath his closed inner-officer door.

She knocked.

Nothing.

She knocked again, louder this time.

His door opened, and when he saw her, he frowned. Not a good sign. Still, he cracked open the outer door.

"Mrs. Peterson. I'm about to go home. If you need legal advice, check with my secretary in the morning."

Funny thing, he didn't meet her gaze.

"Why didn't you tell us the house was haunted?" she blurted. Probably not the wisest thing to do, but there it was.

Startled, he faced her. He even opened his mouth to say something, but nothing came out.

She barged right through the door and into his office, firmly taking a seat. He plodded through like an old man facing execution.

When he finally took his chair behind his desk, he straightened and tried to look lawyerly. He cleared his throat.

"Young lady, I don't know what you mean."

"I think you do. I think you knew but were afraid to tell us. Why? Didn't you think it was important, especially since we wanted to move in?"

He said nothing, simply adjusted his glasses, sat back, then straightened.

"Why don't you tell me what's troubling you."

"Mr. Mathews, please. It's way past the time to be evasive. I've seen the ghost … well, not actually seen him, but I know he's there. I've been to the library and I just left Shirley, Elsie Hall's granddaughter. I know about the rumors. The question is, why didn't you tell us? Didn't you think we had a right to know?"

"I'm a man of facts. I can't support rumors and gossip."

"But still, don't you think you owed us an explanation? Or at least knowledge of the rumors?"

"As Miss Frida's attorney, I owed a fiduciary duty to her, which I performed to the best of my ability. We also had an unbreakable attorney-client privilege, which I also honored. And as a friend to the family for over numerous years, my first duty was to them."

"My husband is part of that family. Doesn't your loyalty extend to him?"

"I'm sorry, Mrs. Peterson. I'll do everything I can to help you regarding the property, but that's as far as I can go."

"Did Eric's grandparents call you the night Frida shot Mr. Halidor? Had you begun your practice yet? It's him, isn't it? He's the ghost."

Mathews gaped at her, then sat back as if wilted. "I'd just graduated when the tragedy occurred. How much do you know?"

She related what Shirley told her. "Is it true? And did Frida think the ghost was her fiancée?"

"What does your husband think?"

"That I'm imagining things."

"Well, then—"

"I'm not and you know I'm not. Please, Mr. Mathews. I want to know if the story is true, and if you think the ghost is Mr. Halidor. If it is, then maybe I can figure out what he wants and how to get rid of him."

"I'm sorry. Attorney-client privilege again and I can't discuss it. You'll have to find your answers elsewhere."

***

On her way home, Lindsay thought about their conversation. While she wasn't an expert on body language, Mathews seldom made eye contact, kept his arms crossed, and turned away from her. Maybe he wasn't actually lying, but he knew more that he would admit. If he wouldn't tell her the details, she had to find someone else to help her. Maybe if she knew the entire story, she could get the ghost to leave.

Just as she stepped onto the front porch, her cell phone rang. Eric. Was she ready to talk to him?

She ignored the ringing, but it rang again and again, demanding she pay attention. Reluctantly, she answered.

"Sorry I haven't called before," he said. "It's been crazy here."

Something in the tone of his voice, a humbling, an unexpected hopelessness caused all her old feelings for him to rush back.

"I understand, honey. I have so much to tell you—"

"Can't talk long. I'm between meetings. Lindsay, I hate to tell you like this, but it's true. Someone's embezzled most of our funds, and if Mark and I can't recover them, we're going down."

As much as she longed to tell everything she'd learned, his distress made her pause. Now wasn't the time to talk about ghosts. Or their troubled marriage.

"Oh honey, I'm so sorry. Can I help? I can hop the next shuttle—"

"No, no, wouldn't do any good. Besides, I'd just worry about you sitting alone in the hotel room while I'm running around like the proverbial chicken with its head cut off. Talk about metaphors. Or is it a simile? And who the fuck cares?"

He never used profanity, so she knew how desperate he must feel.

"What can I do?"

"Just be there. I don't know when I'll be home. It's too expensive to stay in a hotel while the authorities try to track it down, but I can't leave Mark to face it alone. He said I could stay with him, but I'm concerned about you."

"You do what you have to. I'm okay here."

"Thank God for you. I need you to be my anchor right now, something stable to hold onto to."

Anchor? Stable? If he only knew she thought she'd made love to a ghost. But she couldn't tell him, not now, not while he felt his world was coming apart.

"Honey," she said, keeping her voice calm and reassuring, "if worst comes to worst, just remember, we still have each other."

"You didn't sign up for this, a failure husband, a broke one at that, especially if this company goes down."

"Eric, you listen to me. You're not a failure. *You* are what's important. Not the company or the money you make. If the company goes under, we'll be all right. This home is paid for, so we can sell our Palm Springs condo and live here with barely any expenses."

He was silent, listening, so she went on. "Don't worry so much, honey. It's not good for either of us. Do what you must do there, then walk away. Come home. I'll be waiting."

He made a slight sound. Choking back tears? She wished she could give him a reassuring hug.

"I love you," he finally said.

After hanging up, Lindsay sat on the swing, gently pushing, gazing at the lake, wondering, thinking about the possibilities. Should she make the trip anyway?

He'd said something about worrying about her in a hotel, but what if she stayed in their Palm Springs condo? Even though it was about two hours east of Mark and the company quarters, at least Eric could come there and relax when he had the time.

But it was leased for the summer and she couldn't throw out the tenants—especially on a moment's notice.

She could, however, rent a kitchenette motel, one of those for extended stays. She could provide all the wifely things men like such as home-cooked meals and fresh laundry, those little things to help him remember how important he was to her.

But again, it would be costly, and if his company were truly broke, he'd worry about the expense.

She pushed the swing with her foot, watching the sun begin its descent behind the western shore, marveling at the streaks of clouds tinted by brilliant shades of red and gold. Gulls circled and cried overhead, and she realized she'd miss it all if she left.

Should she or should she not? On her android, she checked shuttle flights at the Brainerd airport, and if she hurried, she could make the last one out that evening.

Still, she sat and pushed the swing. Sometime later, she gathered her handbag and keys, entered the house, and paused in the foyer.

Was *he* here?

She waited, but after detecting nothing but normal house smells, she decided to have a sandwich. She could decide afterward whether or not to leave.

She wasn't hesitating because she wanted to learn more about the ghost, was she? It was because her husband asked her to stay.

Wasn't it?

She prepared a ham sandwich and put a dab of potato salad on her plate. Instead of sitting at the corner table, she entered the dining room and kept up the pretense of eating a meal like a normal person by setting the table with silverware and a placemat. She even pulled out her chair, but instead of sitting down, she took half of the sandwich and stood at the window, nibbling and gazing at the ash tree in the growing dusk.

What was it with that tree? How had she known about the carved initials, and why had she reacted so strongly when she saw them?

She felt she knew who the spirit was, and although her suspicions were growing, she didn't know his relationship to her.

Still, it didn't make sense, and even if she did figure it all out, how could such a thing be happening?

While she couldn't answer that, she was no longer afraid.

If only she knew why he haunted the house and what he wanted of her.

After scraping most of her sandwich and salad down the disposal and stacking the plate in the dishwasher, she got ready for bed.

***

They stood in the copse of trees, their private shelter, their kisses deeper, stronger than any they had exchanged before, he kissing her tears away, holding her tighter, consoling each other for strength in the coming days.

"It doesn't have to be this way." He stared into her eyes, begging, pleading.

"I owe too much ..."

He began carving their initials in the tree, far enough from the house to be hidden, yet a lasting declaration of their love. The sun began its descent, yet she watched, transfixed, as he laboriously chipped away at the bark with his knife, loving him so much she wondered if she could survive a life without him.

"There," he said, enclosing the initials with a heart. "No matter what happens, we're joined for all eternity ..."

***

With a sob, Lindsay woke and sat up. The forest was gone. So was he.

More tears welled and she grabbed a tissue from her nightstand. The clock's numbers flipped to 3:00 a.m.

It had been a dream, only a dream. So why was she feeling the woman's heartbreak? Why she did want to go back to sleep and dream of him again, to be with him just one more time?

The woman had been so completely in love. Just looking at him had brought joy beyond anything Lindsay had ever experienced.

Bliss? Not quite. The woman's eyes had been heavy with tears as she imprinted his image into her mind, her heart, knowing he would soon be lost to her.

Still torn from the woman's melancholy, Lindsay grabbed another tissue. She paused. Her eyes widened. *The woman had imprinted his image …*

No, it wasn't possible. Still, she had to find out for sure.

She took the stairs to the attic and to the portrait she had painted.

Chapter Twenty-Three

The image staring back at Lindsay was the man from her dream.

Every instinct told her it was Galen, but how could she have known? How could a man who had died at least sixty years before invade her thoughts, her dreams?

After the first one in which he'd made love to her, she had tried to paint him, but she couldn't remember how he'd looked. But something, *someone*, had guided her strokes. How? By invading her subconscious to lend his memories? That was bizarre, beyond reality. Nevertheless, there it was. She stood before the portrait, knowing she had captured the man from her dream.

Like the woman who had watched him carve the initials, Lindsay gazed lovingly at each feature, at the sadness in his eyes and wanted to kiss it away. Even now, the longing for him pulled at her, causing a fresh wave of tears.

How could she yearn for a man she never knew? If the man in her dream was Galen, then the woman had to be Frida.

Why was she dreaming about two lovers who had lived over sixty years ago?

Knowing she wouldn't sleep the rest of the night, she headed downstairs to the kitchen. Perhaps after some strong coffee she would be better able to figure out what was happening.

Once the entire twelve cups dripped into her carafe, Lindsay filled her mug and took it to the dining room window.

Everything looked so normal. The morning sun was brightening the horizon, painting the forest with a golden light. Squawking crows circled the treetops to claim their branches, and sparrows went about their daily routine. So peaceful, so ordinary.

She spotted the black ash and pictured the initials surrounded by the carved heart. How could she possibly dream about an incident that may or may not have happened to someone else?

But the carved heart *did* exist. How could she explain that?

One possible theory, according to articles and lectures she'd attended in the past, was that she might be sensitive and picking up psychic impressions from the house.

If it were true, she had no idea why it might be happening. She didn't want to know about another person's life; she had enough to handle with her own.

But that explanation was better than the old accusations, allegations she had stamped out and repressed for most of her life, accusations that had made her feel like a freak, like someone so peculiar she didn't deserve to live.

Lindsay sipped her coffee, refusing to give credit to old wounds. But if there was something to psychic impressions, if she had, somehow, entered Frida's mind, her emotions, why was the woman wondering how she could survive a life without her fiancée? They were planning to marry, so why would she lose him? It didn't make sense. She couldn't know then he'd soon die of a gunshot, one from her own hand at that—unless she were planning to kill him. But the woman in the dream had been so in love she'd never even consider harming him. So what had happened?

So many unanswered questions.

She had to find Harry. He might have heard something about Galen and the sisters and what had happened to cause such a tragic outcome. If she could find out more about the sisters, perhaps she could discover why she was so involved in their lives.

With only a passing thought to her husband and his business woes, she hurriedly dressed. She felt slightly hungry but was too impatient to find Harry to spend the time for breakfast. Maybe later she'd stop in the diner where Shirley worked.

Too edgy to walk, she took the car to the library, but it didn't open until ten. Two long hours.

Good Lord, was everything conspiring against her?

She drove the block to Main Street, parked in front of the first diner, rushed in, looked around, and before the young waitress could greet her, spun around and left.

On to the next one. Please, please, Harry. Be there.

But she didn't find him.

Forty-five minutes until the library opened. How could she pass the time without going insane?

Her stomach rumbled, so she stopped at the bakery for coffee and toast. Twenty minutes later, she walked to the library door and peered in. The inside lights were on and Karen Midthun was bent over some paperwork on the counter. This time the door opened.

Lindsay straightened her blouse and ran her hands through her hair. Had she even combed it this morning?

"Good morning," she said. "You may not remember—"

Karen looked up with a smile. "Of course. You're Mrs. Peterson."

"Lindsay, please. I won't keep you long, but I'm looking for Harry Halverson. I thought he might be able to tell me about ..." she trailed off, wondering if she should divulge the true reason.

"About what?" Karen asked helpfully. "Perhaps I can help you."

"He said he knew everyone, and I thought, I thought he could tell me more personal things about the town's history."

"Harry is out of town right now. He just left to visit his son. He goes every year about this time, but I'd be happy to select some books for you."

Lindsay nearly wept with frustration, but she managed to talk to Karen and even left with some books, although she doubted she'd ever read them.

She wandered aimlessly downtown, looking in store windows, not seeing anything. She could call Eric, but while she wondered how he was doing, she couldn't tell him what was happening. He would, she knew, still ridicule her and she couldn't handle that now. She needed someone with whom she could confide, to voice her confusion, her fears.

Two women about her age walked by, talking and laughing, each carrying a package from a local gift shop. Lindsay watched them walk down the street and felt envious. Until she met Eric, she had spent most of her life feeling alone, isolated, as if she were observing people from behind a glass wall.

She wished she had a close friend nearby, but since she'd first arrived in Crosby, too many strange things had been happening to take her time and energy. Plus her concern over her failing marriage. She could admit it now. Her marriage was failing, and she wasn't sure how she felt about it.

Now she wished she had someone for the camaraderie, the sharing of secrets. Just to be able to voice her concerns to someone who cared would be cleansing. But there was no way she could introduce herself to someone. She could just image how that would go:

"Hello, I'm Lindsay Peterson, whose husband inherited Crosby's haunted house, and I'm so sorry I haven't met you before, but you see, I've been so busy with a ghost trying to seduce me and dreaming events from the sisters' lives who lived there before that I haven't had time to join anything or make myself known. But I'm happy to meet you now."

She almost laughed at the mental picture that made.

She had always been a loner, so it wouldn't be new for her to now do the best she could on her own.

Still, she wished she had someone who could help her.

***

In her kitchen, just as she was opening a can of tomato soup, Eric called. He said the normal things such as he missed her, and Lindsay automatically responded.

But did she miss him?

She realized with a start she hadn't given him much thought.

Ever since they had first met, she had hated his business trips and counted the minutes until he called. Now she was listening but not hearing what he was saying, as if his life didn't concern her. And, she had nothing to say to him.

"—and when we confronted him," Eric said, "he finally broke down and admitted he'd taken the money. With some hard work, Mark and I may be able to save the company after all, thank God. It'll mean I'll have to stay another week or two, but it's something I have to do."

"That's good," Lindsay said absently, pouring cream into the can, then adding enough water to fill it. She emptied the liquid into the soup and stirred, wondering if any of the library books had any information she could use.

"It's good I'll have to stay in California?" His tone changed, sounded wary. Wary enough to jar her back to their conversation.

"I meant good you might be able to save the company." She struggled for more to say, to be encouraging. After all, he was her husband, but he wasn't interested in hearing about the strange events happening in her life, so she felt at a loss. She finally asked him about his stay and that got him talking. She made the appropriate responses, and soon after, they hung up.

After pouring her soup into a mug, she crumbled crackers in the mixture and walked into the dining room. Her conversation with her husband had been awkward. Not only did she lie about missing him, but she hadn't even wanted to talk to him. Was she still upset because he hadn't believed her? Of course. She desperately needed an ally, someone who could help her through one of the most difficult times in her life. But it was more than that.

She realized her feelings toward him had changed. While she still felt affection for him, it was a fondness similar to what she could feel toward a brother, uncle, or a friend.

No, she reasoned. A friend would at least listen to her even if he didn't believe her story.

Never would she have thought this would happen. She had been so in love when they'd met.

Something had attracted her from the instant she first saw him, and when he took the empty seat next to her at the donut shop, she had nearly thrown her arms around him. Her reaction shocked her as she had seldom dated and preferred good movies, books, and her art to an active social life. True, he was nice-looking, but that wasn't it. Animal magnetism? Yes, they'd made love many times in the beginning, but that still wasn't it. Thinking back now, she realized she had felt love, just not necessarily physical—which would explain why she wasn't that concerned over their now-sexless marriage.

When he returned home, they'd have to talk, to decide if they wanted to work on their marriage or to end it. But as before, she'd wait for a more appropriate time.

To end her marriage. Never would she have considered she would be the one to fall out of love. But she had, she realized. Her obsession with a man who had lived and died before she was born was shutting out everything else in her life.

She took bites of her soup, the perfect mixture of the rich, tomatoey broth loaded with bits of crunchy saltines, and sought the ash tree. When she found it, she felt as if she were greeting an old friend.

She smiled, remembering the look Galen had given Frida, so filled with love. Frida had gazed at the heart, the initials, and ... her mug halfway to her lips, Lindsay paused. There was something about the initials ... That letter, the first one in the last set of initials, appeared strange for an 'F.' How had it looked? She concentrated, trying to see it better, but it was fuzzy, like dreams usually are. She tried to remember what she had seen that day Eric had led her away, something she hadn't consciously observed.

Think, Lindsay. It's important.

She remembered finding the heart that day, the initials, thinking that on the last set, the first initial she'd assumed was an 'F' looked strange, as if there were more to the faded-out letter. How could there be more to an 'F'?

A sudden idea made her catch her breath. Could that letter have possibly been a 'B'? No, it wasn't possible. Yet it would explain so many things.

She had to check.

She ran to the kitchen, dropped the mug onto the counter, and dashed out the back door. Without worrying about brambles, insects, or anything other than the initials, she cut through the forest to the ash tree. Standing on her toes, she studied the first letter in the last set of initials, tracing the top of the 'F' with her finger. It did extend, and so faded it was barely noticeable, the mark curved back into another curve. A 'B'! GH loves *BP*, the initials read.

Berina Peterson?

How could that be possible?

Galen had been engaged to Frida, not Berina. Yet Lindsay could still see the love on Galen's face when he had looked at the woman, the woman Lindsay assumed was Frida.

Obviously, if she was correct and the 'B' was for Berina, Galen and Berina had fallen in love. If so, that had to be why Frida never married, yet Shirley said Frida shot him. Why? Jealousy?

Lindsay stood back and gazed at the heart, barely comprehending what she had discovered.

Chapter Twenty-Four

Her sister was getting ready for her dancing date at Reindeer Lake with her fiancée, Galen Halidor, and Frida had been in a frenzy all day. Did her new cocktail dress look grown-up enough? After Papa's heavy scowl, Mama had vetoed the black strapless, but had given in when Frida pleaded for a navy blue long-sleeve sheath with a vee neckline. It hugged her body more than Papa wanted, but after all, she argued, she was eighteen now and going to her first adult dance. She certainly didn't want to look like a child.

Berina hadn't met Mr. Halidor, hadn't even seen him. She had been away the past couple of months taking special art classes in Duluth. Papa had refused at first, saying at sixteen, she was too young to stay away from home for two months, but since her mother thought the opportunity would enrich her life, she'd been allowed to go. And if she kept up her grades during her senior year, she could attend next summer as well.

Berina listened as Frida chattered about the corsage Galen would bring, hoping he'd picked up her hints about her dress color. But no matter what, she said, she'd proudly wear it since HE would have given it to her.

Finally, with Tilly, Elsie, Mama, and Berina all helping her get ready—the last minute scramble of pressing out dress wrinkles, picking the right hose shade, her pumps polished after dying them to match her dress—all she had left was to take out the bobby pins and comb her hair, slip on her dress, finish her makeup, and wait.

Berina couldn't wait to see him, this man her sister had fallen for. As the oldest Peterson girl, Frida had dated, of course, but had never talked about marriage. Until now.

Papa approved of the new clerk. As the town's bank president, he said Galen showed promise and was an outstanding young man, the kind of man suitable for his daughter. He was sure, he told the ladies, the young man would propose soon.

Getting married was all Frida talked about, and now, finally, Berina was going to see him. Would she think him as handsome as her sister said?

When he drove up, Mama made Frida stay upstairs in her room, but Berina hurried down the steps to peek out the parlor side window to the driveway. A shiny blue car, a Dodge she thought, since Papa had a newer Dodge, with the chrome sparkling in the sun. He must've spent all day washing and polishing it to impress the family.

When the door opened and he emerged, her world changed forever. Everything else—the grass, the trees—faded away, and she could see nothing but him. Like a god from one of her mythological books, he was the most beautiful man she had ever seen, and his image sealed itself into her mind, her soul.

He towered over the car. A Viking, like Papa's ancestors? Hair the color of the sand on their beach, straight nose, full lips, but it was when he glanced up at the window and saw her that she forgot to breathe.

Mortified at being caught, she felt a hot flush spread all the way to her hair. But she didn't move away.

He grinned, and she was lost.

Squawking crows invaded Lindsay's dream. She opened her eyes to the parlor bright with sunlight, an open book on her lap. She had fallen asleep while reading on the divan. Noooo! She didn't want to let go of Galen, didn't want to lose sight of him.

Maybe if she fell asleep again, she could go back to the dream, back to the way his eyes sparkled with amusement when he'd looked up at the window, the way the gentle breeze from the lake ruffled his hair, and the way his full lips curved when he smiled.

She closed her eyes and willed herself back to the dream, but all she could see was that last glimpse of him when he'd spotted her at the window.

Her? She meant the way he had looked at Berina.

The dream was obviously Berina's first sight of Galen, but why was she dreaming about them? And why she was seeing Galen through Berina's eyes?

Fragments of the old memories surfaced, nearly identical to the dreams she'd been having, and she sat up. She had wondered if she was picking up psychic impressions from Frida, but instead, they must be from Berina.

But would impressions explain the physical contacts she'd experienced since moving in? No matter how Eric had tried to explain them away, she knew in her heart they were real.

And what about her first glimpse of the house with Eric? She had felt as if she were coming home.

How was that possible? While she wouldn't have chosen to be involved in either sister's life, there must be a reason this was happening. Who could help her make sense of it all?

She headed for the kitchen and made a tall glass of iced tea

"You need an exorcist," Shirley had muttered in jest that day at the park.

Maybe the idea wasn't so ridiculous after all. Perhaps not an exorcist, but someone who might have some knowledge of what was happening to her.

Lindsay felt hungry, so she boiled an egg and made egg salad. If Eric were home, he'd want an actual supper instead of a cold sandwich.

She ate her dinner in front of the TV. While scrolling through the channels, a young man and woman in a black and white movie caught her attention and she stopped to watch. They were stepping cautiously through an empty room in an old building, each carrying some type of hand-held equipment, searching for something.

"Is anyone here with us?" the woman asked.

Suddenly, the man and woman looked at each other with surprise and delight.

"Did you hear that?" the woman asked. She glanced at the apparatus she was holding. "I hope it caught the voice."

Voice? Intrigued, Lindsay kept watching and realized they were searching for ghosts. And using their equipment, they said they could actually communicate with the spirit. Was it a movie?

She kept watching until the end, and when she discovered it was a semi-documentary about ghost hunting, she sat up, her sandwich forgotten.

An actual organization that took ghosts seriously enough to search for them! Maybe one would be interested enough to help her.

How to contact them? How did she find anything in today's world? Her laptop!

She ran to her bedroom and, even though she felt a little ridiculous, entered a search for ghost hunting. When several pages appeared, she sat back, astounded at all the information and links. Eagerly she clicked and read, but most were for a popular TV series. That wasn't what she wanted, so she tried again, growing more excited with each find.

After several attempts, she entered Minnesota paranormal societies. When she found several, she felt so excited she entered the number on her cell phone. Just as it began to ring, she hesitated. Eric wouldn't approve and would likely get very upset at the idea.

Yet, she reasoned, he was in California. If she could find an organization interested in her home and get them out to the house before Eric returned, she'd do it.

After contacting three, two as far away as the Twin Cities, describing in an online form what had been happening and why she thought her home was haunted, two contacted her within the hour. Over the phone, she described in more detail the flickering lights, the noises when no one was there, and the Bay Rum scent. She didn't mention the dreams or the personal contacts with the spirit.

The teams from the Minneapolis/St. Paul area were booked until the next month, but Lindsay didn't want to chance Eric would be home, so she booked with the smaller organization in Cass County. They'd be out for the interview and investigation the next evening.

Now to wait.

Finally, she might get some answers.

Chapter Twenty-Five

They were holding each other in the parlor, and she was sobbing, helpless against the upcoming marriage that would take him forever from her arms, and he begging her to stand with him, to tell the truth of their love. Even though she knew she would lose him forever, she couldn't hurt the family that way, not after they had taken her in after she had been abandoned. Even though Frida had only been five and Berina three, she had hugged Berina and forever afterward, loved her as a sister. Berina would be eternally grateful to all the Petersons for loving her.

Galen kissed her again, and this time, she kissed him back with all the desperate passion she had held inside. She allowed him further liberties, she, longing to know the joy of love fulfilled before it was lost, helped him free the buttons of her robe. He caressed her breasts and she closed her eyes in ecstasy, but just before they became one, she heard Frida, shouting and running down the stairs. Galen jumped up and stood over her, to shield her, then ... an explosion so loud her ears rang, another one, then another, blood, so much blood. She reached for him as he lay in all that blood, holding him, desperately trying to pass some of her life force to him. After two barely audible words, he sighed and was gone …

Lindsay's own screams jerked her awake. Her heartbeat pulsing in her temples, she sat up, her frantic gaze seeking Galen. Sobbing, she reached for him, desperate to hold him, to feel him next to her one last time, but … there was nothing.

He had gone. Disappeared.

So had the parlor.

She scanned the room. What was happening? Where was she?

As her eyes adjusted in the moonlit night, her sobs dwindled to gulps and she began to see. Her novel on the bedside table. Amber numbers glowed on a digital clock. 5:20 a.m. She stared dully at it until the realization of who and where she was slowly returned.

It had been a dream, but not the one she had hoped for. This soul-wrenching horror left her suspended between two worlds.

But the love she'd felt still lingered, love such as she'd never before known.

And he had died in her arms.

As dawn lightened the room several hours later, she was still awake. She hadn't dared to go back to sleep, afraid she'd dream about his last moments again. Even now, the loss was so crushing she could barely take the next breath.

"Oh, Galen …"

She had to see him once more, had to look into the eyes that had seen into her soul.

She ran to the attic and to the portrait she had painted, and as soon as she entered, the room filled with the scent of Bay Rum. All her senses opened to receive him as the morning glory opens to the sun.

"Yes, yes …"

Her gaze caressed his image, hungrily taking it in, letting it fill her center. She traced the curve of his lips and closed her eyes, wanting to feel his warm mouth on hers once again, on her breasts, and she wanted more—the fulfillment of his body next to hers.

But that was never to be.

Weeping, she fell to her knees and curled onto the floor. Warmth surrounded her, the familiar scent comforting her like a favorite blanket. She drew it in and, like a child grieving over a lost treasure, cried herself to sleep.

Sometime later, the musical jingle from her cell phone downstairs woke her. She didn't feel like talking to anyone, not even her husband, so she let it ring, hoping it would stop. But after her cell quit, the landline in the kitchen rang and rang until the voice mail picked it up. It was Eric, his voice worried.

She sat up, and while she had no energy to rush downstairs, she called him back a few minutes later.

"Sorry, I was asleep."

"You don't sound well. Is everything all right?"

She'd stayed up to finish a novel, she told him, then fell asleep. And how was he? How were the proceedings going? That was all it took for him to launch into a monologue about the company, and even though she had a difficult time responding, he seemed satisfied with her occasional one-syllable responses. After a short while, he signed off with a quick "love you."

Too drained to bother dressing, Lindsay brewed coffee, but after the first cup, the acid rose in her throat. She made some dry toast and opened a diet soda, knowing the fizz would settle her stomach.

She took her glass, and simply holding and munching the toast, sat at the dining table and gazed at the black ash. From her vantage point, she could only glimpse the top, but knowing it was there drew comfort.

Why were the dreams, if they were dreams, coming more frequently now? To have dreamed about Galen's death was something she never wanted to experience again.

Why he still lingered in the house, she didn't know. She had read about the white light people saw after death, and if it were true, why hadn't he passed through it?

So many questions. But one of the most puzzling was how she, Lindsay, who had never been out of

California, wound up with Eric at that house in Minnesota—and a ghost.

It all seemed so ridiculous. Some of the old feelings from her childhood intruded, and even though she knew the initials were real, she couldn't help the doubts that stole her reasoning and made her wonder about her sanity.

Maybe the investigative team would be able to help her, at least witness if there truly was a ghost and it wasn't all her imagination. She hoped they could answer her questions. If they could, would the dreams stop?

They had to; she didn't know if she could survive another night like the one she'd just experienced.

Yet she'd give everything in her life to feel him next to her just one more time.

Why, Galen? Why is this happening to me?

Something about the dream … something she needed to know, but it was just beyond her grasp.

Then she remembered. His last words. Two of them. What were they? If she could remember, she might know why all this was happening.

She heard a sound—a male voice, faint, as if from far away—the same words from her dream:

"I'll wait."

***

At dusk, a car pulled in the driveway. Three women and a young man emerged from a light gray SUV, so Lindsay stepped out to the porch to welcome them.

A slim, fortyish woman in jeans, her honey-colored hair nearly to her waist, stepped forward and offered her hand.

"I'm Katie Foreman, and this is my team." She introduced her assistant, Sharon, who seemed around her age, and Joyce, the tech specialist, a little older. Ken towered over everyone, his facial fuzz revealing he was still a teenager. All had tote bags slung over their shoulders. "Thank you for allowing us into your home."

"I'm so happy you could get here so quickly," Lindsay said, leading them into the house. "As I told you on the phone, I need your help."

Katie hesitated in the foyer and exchanged a knowing glance with Sharon, and when they entered the parlor, both investigators paused.

"Here's where it happened," Sharon said, and Katie nodded.

"Sharon's claircognizant," Katie explained to her client. "That's the ability to know things. I'm more of an empath, which means I just know, or feel, the emotions of the spirit. I'd like to take a few moments and talk to the spirit, to let him know we're not here to harm him or try to force anything he doesn't want."

Fascinated, Lindsay watched as Katie walked to the center of the room. Her team grew quiet.

"Hello," Katie said, turning in all directions. "I'm Katie, and I want you to know that my team and I want to help you, that we're not here to harm you in any way. We have equipment to receive any messages you might have for us or for the owner, Lindsay Peterson." She went silent as if waiting. Then she shook her head. "I'm not getting anything from him, but if it helps, I don't feel he's a threat."

Lindsay had known that in her heart, but it was good to have Katie confirm it.

Joyce took a piece of equipment from her tote.

"An EMF meter," Katie explained while Joyce held it and moved it slowly in the air. Nearly square, the blackish instrument had a digital readout at the top. "It measures electromagnetic fields in the area."

Lindsay frowned. "I don't understand."

"The theory is that spirits draw energy from the surroundings to manifest, and when one is present, it gives off an electromagnetic field which can be measured. The higher the energy, the stronger the presence."

"One point zero three," Joyce called out, waving the instrument at different levels, "two point three four."

Ken silently texted on his android.

"We'll check for wiring and fuse boxes to make sure we're not picking up readings from normal household currents," Katie told him, then turned to Lindsay. "Which reminds me. Thanks for avoiding perfume or scented lotions this evening. Some of our women clients forget, and it's difficult to detect phantom smells."

"If he shows up, you won't have a problem with his scent."

"The Bay Rum you mentioned," Katie confirmed. She looked around the room. "Where's a good place to put our equipment, somewhere easily accessed during the investigation?"

"How about the dining room table? It's big enough." Lindsay led the team into the dining room where they unloaded their bags onto the table. She noticed several cameras, two-way radios, and other pieces of equipment she didn't recognize.

"Why not show us the hot spots?" Katie suggested. "Places you've seen something unusual. Shadows perhaps, or flickering lights."

Lindsay led the team through the rooms where the scent had been the strongest—the foyer, parlor, dining room, bedroom, the attic, and even the bathroom. Ken followed closely, his fingers flying on his android.

"His way of taking notes," Katie explained with a smile. "He texts faster than he can write."

Ken reddened, shrugged, then after the tour, he busied himself placing video cameras in the rooms with the most activity.

Lindsay led them back to the parlor for the refreshments she'd prepared. Even though Katie had told her over the phone it wasn't necessary, the team thanked her for the cut fruit, chips, nuts, water, and colas. Ken quietly devoured everything the rest of the team hadn't grabbed and looked as if he could down several more plates. Lindsay liked his gentle nature and considered making some sandwiches for him.

Just as she opened the fridge, Katie spoke.

"It'll be dark soon," she addressed the team, "so let's make sure everything's in working order." Everyone checked batteries in their flashlights and the other equipment.

"One way we first suspect a spirit is present is when our batteries die," she told Lindsay. "Since they need energy to manifest, they drain energy from batteries and other power sources. That's why you'll often see flickering lights, although they sometimes do that to get your attention."

About fifteen minutes later, Katie stood. "Okay, we're ready. Ken, get the lights."

Chapter Twenty-Six

"You turn out the lights just like on the TV program," Lindsay remarked.

"The darkness tends to heighten our senses," Katie told her, selecting a flashlight and one other instrument. "And for some reason we haven't fully realized, spirits seem to gather more energy after dark."

Lindsay helped Ken with the house lights, then they joined the team in the dining room. Each member picked a flashlight and at least one other device. Ken took the digital camera.

"A cool camera," he said. "Modified for the full spectrum of light people can't see."

"You might actually get a photo of the ghost?"

"Sure, but it doesn't always happen. If it does, don't expect to see someone's shape. It's usually a blur. You'll see—if they're here and if they want to be seen." As if he'd run out of breath, he grew quiet and busied himself with the camera.

Of course Galen would want to be seen. He'd made himself known to Lindsay ever since she first appeared on the property, so he couldn't have any objection to being seen—even if it was just a blur. It would be proof he was there, proof she wasn't being ridiculous as Eric had said. Evidence that there truly was someone or something causing the touches and caresses she'd felt, someone behind the dreams and whisperings she'd been hearing. Proof she wasn't going insane.

"Should I stay here," she asked Katie, "or is it okay if I go with you?"

"Whatever you prefer, but make sure your phone's off. Same with your TV. We don't want contamination from background noise."

"Give me five minutes." The TV wasn't on, but Lindsay checked her cell and the house phone's ringer, then ran back to the parlor hoping she hadn't missed anything.

Katie had selected two pieces of equipment. "I'll start with these."

The first device was rectangular in shape with a digital readout at the top. "An EVP recorder— electronic voice phenomenon. If we're lucky, we may be able to pick up a word or two from the spirit. We can't always hear them with our ears, but if they say something, the recorder will pick it up and we can hear when we play it back."

"You can actually hear the spirit talking?"

"If he or she chooses to speak."

His voice. Lindsay could almost hear it again, the deep, rich tones that dipped even lower when they'd gazed into each other's eyes and he'd moaned her name, the voice that had whispered words of a love that would never die. More than anything, she wanted to hear it again, but how would she react? She supposedly was this harried homeowner plagued with a haunting. If she heard him speak, would she be able to maintain that façade, or would she crumble with love and longing like an adolescent schoolgirl swooning over a teen idol?

But it didn't matter. Nothing mattered except hearing his voice. She felt the desperate need rising until she trembled with excitement.

Katie picked up another device about the size of a cordless phone, gray with five colored strips—two greens, a yellow, orange, and red. Each led to a button on the edge. "A K2 meter," she explained. "Measures shifts in energy levels around us. When a spirit is present, a buzzer and a light display lets us know. If we're very lucky, we can communicate with the spirit."

"How?"

"You'll see it if it happens."

For the next hour, two teams took turns moving through the house while Joyce monitored the video camera from the dining room computer. Katie and Lindsay went first, beginning with the downstairs. To Lindsay's disappointment, everything stayed pretty quiet—the foyer where she'd first noticed the Bay

Rum scent, the dining room window where she'd heard faint whisperings.

"Don't get discouraged," Katie said. "It's early, and we still have the upstairs to investigate."

Lindsay hoped Galen would manifest upstairs, or at least reveal himself in a way the team could detect. But there was nothing. Not in the bathroom where she'd felt his presence in the tub, nor in her bedroom where she'd dreamed of life in the past. No scent, no fluctuating meter readings, nothing. Lindsay tried not to show her frustration, but Katie must have sensed it.

"It's okay. We may or may not get anything tonight. It just depends on what the spirit wants."

"But I don't understand. I was sure he'd want to let us know he's here."

She paused. Was she sure he'd want that? She had been so positive he would show himself in some way, show some kind of proof he was there. But he had not. Why?

Was he hiding? Or simply not there? She nearly cried with disappointment.

Then it hit her. Maybe Galen didn't want proof. Maybe he only wanted to communicate with her. While she could understand, she had desperately wanted to hear his voice.

"Oh, Galen ..."

Katie looked sharply at her. "You know the spirit?"

By this time, Lindsay no longer cared if Katie knew more. It might even be better. Someone had to know enough to help her.

"I think it may be the former owner's fiancée." She explained what Shirley had told her, still with no mention of her physical contacts with the ghost, and certainly nothing about a past life. "I know he must want something, but if he doesn't appear tonight, I don't know how to find out."

Katie listened quietly. "If the spirit chooses to not make himself known tonight, I have another suggestion for you—if you're interested."

"Anything."

"Make an appointment for a private reading. You could make it with Sharon, me, or another medium, but you might discover more than tonight's investigation might reveal."

At this point Lindsay was desperate enough to try anything. "Thanks. I'll do that."

Katie nodded. "Since we're all here now, let's continue with tonight's investigation. We'll take a break and let Sharon and Ken have a turn. Who knows, the spirit may surprise us yet."

At the dining room table, Lindsay felt too edgy to sit. She had something to drink, then watched the computer screen with Joyce. Everything was quiet, too quiet, and Lindsay was losing hope.

The other team made their way back to the dining room. Sharon shook her head.

"I don't understand why nothing's happening," Lindsay, near tears, said to Katie. "I'm sorry I wasted your time."

"On-site experience is never wasted. And you're welcome to call us if activity begins again." The team began to dismantle their equipment. Katie silently gazed at Lindsay. "Off the record, though, I think you're right."

"I agree," Sharon said. "Something *is* here. Male."

"Do you get anything else?" Katie asked.

"Just flashes," Sharon said, "but they're quickly gone. He's not willing to reveal himself."

Lindsay nodded, afraid that if she spoke, she'd break down.

"Look," Katie turned to Lindsay. "If you've felt his presence, why not say something to him now? It might encourage him to reveal himself in some way."

As much as she would love to talk to him, to ask him why he was silent, Lindsay felt uncomfortable doing so in front of someone else.

Still, it was worth a try. At least these people believed her.

"Hello," she said awkwardly. After an encouraging nod from Katie, she continued, still ill at ease, but her voice grew stronger. "Galen, are you here? Why won't you talk to me?"

Katie checked the EVP recorder. "Maybe we'll get something."

They both waited a few moments, but nothing happened.

Then, they heard a slight thump from upstairs. Katie and Lindsay exchanged glances. It sounded again, louder this time. They headed for the stairs, but on the second-floor landing, they heard nothing more. They waited. Just as Lindsay was giving up hope, a slight Bay Rum scent wafted from the attic.

"He's here!" Lindsay took to the stairs with Katie close behind.

They rushed into the room, and Katie used her flashlight to search the area. Even as they stood, the Bay Rum scent grew stronger.

"Smell it?" Lindsay asked.

Katie whispered into her two-way radio. "Everyone to the attic. *Now*."

Lindsay walked the room, her arms spread joyfully. "You're here, you're finally here."

When Katie's flashlight beam hit the painting, she stepped in front of it.

"You did this?" She studied it. "It's him, isn't it? You've seen him."

"In dreams …"

"It's him."

Sharon, followed by the other two members, spilled into the attic. The scent was strong now, and Ken made frantic notes.

"Thank you, thank you," Lindsay whispered.

Moonlight from the window didn't dispel the shadows. The temperature dropped.

"Man, it's dark in here." Sharon pointed her EMF meter in different directions and read off the increasing numbers.

Joyce walked the room holding a small instrument with a reddish tip. She stopped in the northwest corner near the portrait. "We've got a cold spot, nearly a twenty-degree drop."

"An infrared thermometer," Katie told Lindsay. "Theory is when a spirit/ghost tries to manifest, it draws heat energy around the area and that causes a cold spot."

"Something moved," Sharon said. "In that corner." She directed her flashlight beam to the northwest corner. Ken started filming, scanning the room with his camera.

"Let's try an EVP session." Katie activated the K2 meter.

Chapter Twenty-Seven

"Is anyone here?" Katie asked, watching the LED buttons on her K2 meter.

Lindsay moved close, her eyes on the meter. But even though the scent had grown stronger, the device showed no response.

"Who are you?" Katie asked. "Why are you here? Is there anything you'd like to say to the owner?"

Still nothing.

"Galen," Lindsay murmured. "Please …"

The meter sprang to life. All five LED buttons blazed with light, blinking in rotation several times before stopping.

"We got him," Katie whispered to Lindsay. A series of flashes from behind Katie lit up the room. Without turning, Katie whispered to Ken, "Did you set up a video camera in here?"

"Didn't have enough, but maybe I'll get something on the digital."

Katie addressed the room again. "Thank you for responding. The homeowner thinks you may be a gentleman who died in this house. Is that true?"

No response. She tried again.

"Will you talk to us?"

Still nothing.

"We don't want to hurt you. We just want to know who you are and why you're here."

Lindsay couldn't seem to look away from the LED lights, and the lack of response was devastating. She'd hoped to learn why he lingered in the house and more about her connection to him, but he didn't seem to want to cooperate.

"A male spirit is in the room with us," Sharon murmured.

Lindsay stepped to the portrait. "Why won't you communicate with us? Please, I need to know …"

The K2 went wild again.

"Looks like he'll only respond to you, Lindsay, so go ahead. Talk to him. Ask questions and we'll see if he answers."

"He might answer? How?"

Katie indicated the meter. "If he'll cooperate, we hope to communicate with him through it."

She turned to the crew. "Okay guys, turn off all equipment." She explained to Lindsay, "That's to eliminate other possible frequency sources."

She cleared her throat and held out the K2 meter. "Lindsay wants to talk to you, and with this piece of equipment, you can communicate with her."

The first button, green, briefly lit with a faint glow. Then it was gone.

"I'll have Lindsay talk to you, but first, to make sure we can communicate, would you light up the meter for me now?"

Nothing happened.

"I understand you want to talk to Lindsay, but if you'll light up the meter now, once for 'yes' and twice for 'no,' we'll know it's you and not a malfunction. Then she'll talk to you. Do you understand?"

Everyone concentrated on the K2, and for a moment, nothing happened. Then, like plugging in Christmas tree lights, all the LED buttons lit up.

"Just to make sure, am I talking to the spirit present in this house?" Again, everyone watched the lights. And again, they all lit up.

He was going to talk. Lindsay hadn't noticed she'd been holding her breath until the meter lit up.

"Thank you," Katie said. "I'll turn it over to Lindsay now." The meter lit once. Katie showed Lindsay how to keep the device activated.

Lindsay had so many questions that her mind felt in a jumble. She wanted to know everything, but she couldn't keep Katie's team that long, nor could she be certain Galen would fully cooperate. But as she'd learned when beginning to paint, stick to the basics.

"Are you Galen?"

After a slight pause, the meter lit once. A surge of joy rippled through her.

"Why are you here? What do you want?"

The meter lit once, then twice, then once again. Lindsay looked questioningly at Katie.

"Just ask yes or no questions," she said. "He can't answer any other way."

Of course. Lindsay tried again. "Did you die in this house?"

The meter answered once.

"I'm sorry," Lindsay said. "Was it natural causes?"

No.

Lindsay paused, wondering how to phrase the next question. "Was someone in my husband's family responsible?"

Yes.

A coldness rippled through Lindsay. His answers coincided with her dreams, and while they were confirmation that it wasn't all her imagination, it was frightening in a way. Yet she had to continue, had to know what was happening.

"Is that why you're here? Revenge on the house— or someone?"

No.

"Do you want to harm me? Or my husband?"

No.

"Are you causing the strange things that have been happening to me?"

Yes. No. Yes. No.

"I don't understand." She turned to Katie. "Do you know what this means?"

"Maybe he can't answer that. Ask another question and see what you get." She paused. "Ken, are you getting all this?"

"Yeah." No longer snapping pictures, the young man was busy with his notes.

Lindsay wondered how to ask the next question, the one at the heart of everything that had been happening since moving to the house.

"Do you know me?"

All lights on the K2 began a series of rotations, finally going dim. Then it lit once.

Yes.

"Twenty milligausses," Katie said to Ken. "Be sure and note that."

"Is that good?" Lindsay asked.

"It's a strong response."

"Camera died," Ken said.

"Mine too," Joyce added.

"Energy drain," Katie told Lindsay. "Do you have more questions for him?"

Only a couple million questions, Lindsay thought. She had an important one but wasn't sure how to ask, especially in front of the others.

"Do I know you?"

Katie cut a questioning glance at her client, but Lindsay kept watch on the meter. This was the key to everything that had been happening, but to her disappointment, there was no response.

"The spirit may have left," Katie said.

Sharon whispered. "He's still here, but he's fading."

No, he can't leave now. "Galen, please don't leave."

"Try asking in a different way," Katie suggested.

"Did we know each other ... before?"

Again the sharp glance from Katie.

Lindsay waited for a response, but again nothing happened.

"Galen, please. I need to know."

Finally, one faint answer.

Yes.

Lindsay stared at the button. Excitement surged through her. It was true. Her dreams were based on reality.

A familiar buzzing vibrated in her right ear, as if someone were speaking in a range she couldn't perceive.

"I heard something," Sharon said, plugging in her headphone to the EVP recorder. "Can you speak again?"

Again Lindsay heard the sound. "What? I don't understand."

"I got it! Let me make sure." Listening intently through her headphone, Sharon played it back, punched some buttons, then handed the recorder and headphones to Katie. "See if you hear the same thing."

Katie listened. "That was clear! Definitely a Class A EVP. I'll play it for you, Lindsay. It's only a couple of words, but I think you'll be able to understand them." She punched the speaker button.

Static filled the room, but then a voice spoke over the noise. A faint one, but distinct. The voice she'd heard in her dreams. *His* voice.

An all-consuming joy spread warmth through her body. Tears tumbled down her cheeks.

It was Galen.

"Are you all right?"Katie asked, taking a tissue from her jean's pocket.

"More than all right." Dabbing her eyes, Lindsay smiled. "Play it again, please. I couldn't make out the words."

Katie hit the button, and this time Lindsay caught the enunciation. He spoke two words, the same two he'd whispered as he lay dying of gun shots, the promise he made to her as she cradled him in her arms, begging him not to leave her.

"I'll wait."

Chapter Twenty-Eight

Katie's crew packed to leave, congratulating each other on the evening's successful investigation. Off to the side, apart from the conversation, Lindsay silently watched. While she had suspected the truth, tonight's session had been overwhelming.

Galen, the man from her dreams, was real. And they knew, or had known, each other. Her dreams were factual, which meant, she realized, her whimsical stories as a child were based on fact.

There could only be one explanation—a former life, a life lived in this house.

Reincarnation.

Memories she had spent a lifetime pushing away flooded back, the adult voices speaking to her child's mind. What she was telling them wasn't rational, they'd said, shaking their heads in pity, followed by doctor's appointments, the threat of institutionalization if she ever spoke of such things again.

And she hadn't. Eventually the visions had faded.

Early in her adult life, she had toyed with the theory of reincarnation, had even bought some books on the subject seeking something, some explanation for what she had experienced. But with the voices of the adults from her young world still echoing in her mind, the idea that she had been born again into a new life had seemed ludicrous.

But now she wondered. How else could she explain the déjà vu she'd experienced the first time she saw the house and everything that had happened afterward? Even though it was beginning to make sense, she still found it incredible.

Visions? Dreams?

Reincarnation?

But, she thought, the old doubts returning, if it were reincarnation, if she had been Berina, why didn't she remember the woman's life during her waking hours?

She did remember: the posey wallpaper, going to the outhouse. Certain segments of Berina's life were coming back, just not everything.

Dare she believe? Even if she did, how would she explain it to Eric? Although it wasn't a laughing matter, she smiled, picturing his reaction.

She must have made a sound as both Katie and Sharon stopped their packing to look at her.

"I was just thinking of my husband's reaction to all this," she explained with a sad smile. "He already thinks I've lost it. If I tell him I had a ghost hunter investigate the house, he'll certainly be convinced I've gone off the deep end."

"That's a common reaction," Katie said, "and you're in a tough spot. I wish I could help, but while the team can sometimes record evidence of a haunting, I can't advise clients how to deal with it—except to try to understand."

Lindsay had no answer.

"Or," Sharon said, "if they prefer, arrange for an exorcism."

"Force him out?" That hadn't even occurred to her. Did she want him to go? Even though it would certainly help her marriage, she realized she didn't want Galen to leave.

God, how warped was she to prefer a ghost to her husband?

"You have another option," Katie said. "As I mentioned before, you might wish to try and contact the spirit further through a medium."

"Would I be able to learn more about him? And about my relationship with him?"

"It's possible, but not guaranteed," Sharon said. "We can try."

Katie quietly studied Lindsay. "There's more at play here than a simple haunting, isn't there? As if a haunting could ever be simple."

Sudden tears tumbled down Lindsay's cheeks and she couldn't speak. Embarrassed, she ran into the kitchen for a tissue, a paper towel, anything.

Katie followed.

"I'm sorry," Lindsay managed, trying to stem the flow. "I don't know why I'm crying."

"It's all right. It's been quite a night, and I'm sure your emotions are all over the place."

"It's just, just …" Fresh tears appeared.

Katie, her arms around her client, gently led her to a chair.

"Try to relax and let yourself adjust to what's happened. You've been through quite a lot, you know."

"You have no idea how much."

"I wish I could help."

"You mentioned a private session. I might try that."

"I don't know anything about you or your relationship with the spirit, and I don't want to pry, but obviously he seems to know you. Perhaps he has something he wants you to know, some message he wants to pass on to you, and a personal reading could be helpful."

Should she tell Katie what she truly suspected? It would be such a relief to confide in someone, someone who believed the implausible was possible.

"If I'm right," she began, "I knew the spirit … Galen, before."

Katie pulled out the chair next to her client and sat. "Before you were married? Was he a former lover, maybe one who doesn't want to let go?"

"I wish it were that simple." Lindsay barely took a breath. "I think I knew him … in a former life." She paused, waiting for Katie's reaction. If the investigator believed her, she could possibly help, but if not, if she dismissed it like everyone else had always done, Lindsay would be more alone than ever.

She searched Katie's eyes, intent on hers. What would she say?

"I see." Katie sat back in her chair.

Lindsay felt as if her soul were weeping. "You don't believe me."

"It's not that I don't believe you. I hadn't expected anything like that, so I'm thinking how best to help you."

Lindsay kept her eyes on the investigator, clinging to her words as if she were sucked into a whirlpool and Katie her rescuer.

"Reincarnation is a doctrine followed by more people than you might aware of," Katie began, "and it's grown in popularity in the past few decades. I think the best advice I can offer is to do some research. Read about Hinduism, the Buddhists, and other religions that practice the belief. Find out why they believe as they do."

"Then you believe in reincarnation?"

"My personal belief is not the question. Instead, you need to find answers to your dilemma, although I'm not certain it's a dilemma. Most people who've remembered their past lives have found the experience enriching, sometimes an answer for phobias, for likes and dislikes in their present life."

"Phobias aren't my problem. I'm discovering I've lived a former life with this ghost, this man. For what purpose? Am I supposed to learn something from realizing I knew him in a former life? All it's done is make me grieve over our lost lives and long for him now. I'm a married woman who wants a ghost rather than her husband. How do I deal with that *now*?"

"You must not make the mistake of sacrificing your present life with the one you've already lived, no matter how much you loved this man. Remember, Lindsay, you have this life to live now. Knowing about your past can enrich this life."

Lindsay's voice was barely a whisper. "But what if my past life was better?"

"Was it truly? Was your former life better than the one you're living now?"

Lindsay didn't answer. While she longed for Galen in the flesh, she also remembered the heartbreak of clandestine meetings, of knowing he couldn't be hers, and of finally, the agony of watching him die.

But wasn't having him, even for a short time in her former life, better than enduring this life without him?

"I'm not sure."

"If you're that uncertain, I suggest you work to change your present life." Her expression somber, Katie continued. "Life is a precious gift, not to be taken lightly. We all have a purpose, so work, study, try to find the meaning of this life you have today." She paused. "I know this must be difficult for you, and I'll try to help all I can. The spirit in this house desires communication with you, and through him, I see images of two people stealing moments together, two young people deeply in love. While I can't promise results, perhaps I'll be able to see more during a session. Then perhaps you will know what to do." She handed Lindsay her card. "Call when you're ready."

Lindsay studied the card as if it alone could answer her questions.

"We all have a purpose in life you know," Katie said. "Perhaps together, we can discover yours."

***

Lindsay placed the card into the silverware drawer so she wouldn't lose it. She already knew she'd make an appointment, but she needed some time to adjust to everything that had happened that night.

Later, after everyone had left, she poured a glass of wine and took it to her bedroom. If only she could relax and logically sort things enough to form a plan of action.

She decided to read everything she could on the subject, but at the moment she felt too consumed with the wonder of it all to worry about theories and whether they could be proven.

A former life in this house …

… as Berina.

Would she eventually remember everything about that life? She couldn't answer that, and right now she wasn't certain it was crucial to remember everything.

She thought of Frida, and for a heartbeat in her erratic memory, she could see the look on her sister's face that terrible night when Frida realized whom she'd shot. And with that realization came the knowledge that she, Berina, had betrayed her.

Lindsay wished it had been different, and while she didn't consciously remember, she knew from Eric and the attorney that Frida had cared for her, Berina, until she died.

Why? Shouldn't it have been the other way around?

She sipped her wine and drew her bath, wishing she knew the answer. But knowing wouldn't change her love for Galen, either in the past or today.

Adding lavender salts, she longed for his arms, and at that instant, she knew her relationship with Eric was over. When a woman prefers a ghost to her husband, there's not much chance of a happy marriage.

She just hoped he didn't come home before she could process everything, one way or the other.

She stepped into the tub, thinking of that evening Galen had begun to make love to her right after she and Eric had moved in. Before she'd realized it wasn't her husband, she had become passionately aroused.

"Galen." Even saying his name sent a delicious shiver through her body.

She was totally, madly in love—with a ghost.

Once in bed, she left on the lamp … just in case.

Would she dream of her lover tonight? If she did, please God, let it be of any time other than of that horrific last evening.

Chapter Twenty-Nine

Something woke Lindsay and she opened her eyes to total darkness. The bedside light had gone out and the moon had disappeared.

All her senses alert, she lay wondering what had disturbed her sleep. Was it Galen? Would he appear to her tonight?

She sat up and scanned the blackness. "Galen? Are you here?"

Only silence answered her. And not a trace of Bay Rum.

After a few moments of waiting, hoping he'd appear, she lay back down and closed her heavy eyes. After such an emotional evening, she desperately needed sleep.

Still, something was wrong. But what?

She listened to the still night. And realized it was too still. No frogs, no crickets, nothing.

She sat up and strained to listen. But there was no sound except for her heart pounding in her temples.

Then she heard it. A soft splash from the lake, a sound different from a jumping fish or a turtle. Something unusually large was breaking the surface, yet it didn't sound as if it were rising and flopping back into the water; instead, the splash was quieter, as if whatever it was could glide through the water without attracting attention.

The lake creature?

She rubbed her eyes. Was this strange sound part of a dream? Was she dreaming now?

The splash sounded again, so, dream or not, she padded to the front bedroom overlooking the lake.

Pushing the drapes aside, she searched the water below. The moon slipped behind streaked clouds, and all she could see were vague outlines in the dim light. But directed by a slight splash, she spotted a dark outline in the center of the lake directly in front of the house. Even while she watched, an elongated head with a slim neck rose about four to five feet above the surface, water dripping from its snout.

Kahnah'bek?

She couldn't believe what she was seeing.

In only her tee and panties, she flew downstairs and down the porch steps to the shore, her bare feet racing over grass, sand, and pebbles. On the beach, she caught a slight fishy odor. The night was so dark she could barely make out features, but there, right before her, the creature of legends appeared. She stared in awe, too entranced to be frightened. It made a slight blowing sound as if it were clearing water from its nostrils, then turned its head and looked directly at her.

"Hello," she whispered, then realized what a ridiculous thing to do.

The creature stared a moment more then soundlessly sank beneath the water. A large flipper appeared, then submerged as the creature rolled or turned in a different direction. Hundreds of bubbles rose to the surface, faded, then the water was calm again.

Her heart racing, Lindsay stood several minutes to see if it would reappear, but when the moon came out of hiding, it revealed nothing unusual on the lake waters. The frogs, crickets, and insects resumed their nightly chorus, and a mosquito landed on her neck, another on her arm. Slapping them, she ran back to the house.

She had actually seen the fabled lake creature.

What should she do? Call the sheriff? Would they believe her? And if they did, would they hunt it down and kill it?

Is that what she wanted?

The creature had looked right at her and didn't try to harm her. It simply disappeared below the surface.

The creature. She'd call and tell Eric the legend was true, that she had actually seen it. He would be asleep, but this was too exciting not to share.

She headed for the house phone in the parlor, then hesitated. Oh sure, she'd could imagine his reaction to a call in the middle of the night. She'd tell him she'd seen the monster and then tell him not only did his ancestral home house a ghost, but she had lived before as his aunt.

He'd certainly believe all that.

Maybe she'd keep it all to herself just a little longer.

Just as she entered her room, she paused. The room was different, the air thicker. The hairs on her arms prickled.

Cautiously she entered, looking all around. Was it Galen? Would he finally appear?

She made her way to her bed, slowly, afraid to make a sudden move. If he were here, she didn't want to startle him or force him away. When she reached to turn on the lamp, a spark of static sizzled and she jerked back.

Bay Rum filled the air.

"Don't turn it on," a male voice said, *his* voice, the voice her heart would know even if an eternity separated them.

"Galen?" Joyously, she turned around.

To an empty room.

"Noooo," she cried. "I know you're here. Why can't I see you?"

"Berina, my darling. I've waited so long …" His voice sent delight through her body. Finally, they would be together. Nearly weeping, she whirled in the direction of his voice.

Still nothing.

"Where are you?" she cried in desperation. "Why can't I see you? Please, Galen, I want to see you, see your eyes, your lips." She felt the stirring of air, the slight shift in pressure and knew he was near. Her longing for him grew so intense she could barely breathe.

"I can't allow that," he said. "It is too dangerous for you."

"What are you talking about? Please, Galen, I must feel you, hold you in my arms."

"I want more than anything to be with you, but this must be enough for us."

"What are you saying? I don't understand."

"Think, my darling, each time I came to you in dreams, you woke a little more exhausted. Being with me in this state is draining your life force."

"I don't care. You must understand how I feel, how I long to see you, to touch you."

"As I long for you. Now I must go before I sacrifice your life for my own pleasure. It's enough of a miracle to just speak to you. Goodbye, my darling, until I can return …"

She felt a whisper of touch on her eyelids, the tip of her nose, then her lips. The touch grew faint, and the air pressure wavered.

"No, don't leave! Please!" The scent dissipated and she knew he had gone. "Galen," she cried, falling onto the bed, weeping uncontrollably.

That couldn't be all that was allowed. The heavens wouldn't be that cruel. There had to be a way.

"Galen? Are you here?"

But there was no answer. She had to see him, so she headed for the attic.

God, she really was going mad, but she lay her cheek against the canvas, wanting with all her heart to take him into her arms.

***

When her cell phone woke her, the sun was flooding the attic with brilliant light. As before, she ignored it until it stopped, and again, the house phone rang. She rose stiffly from the floor, made her way to her bedroom where she listened to Eric's voicemail about his move to Mark's home.

Her eyes heavy, she listlessly carried the phone to the kitchen and made coffee. Once she had downed two cups, she returned his call. Not that she wanted to talk to him, but it was better than trying to explain why she didn't answer or didn't call.

"You sound strange," he said after telling Lindsay about his move. She had responded very little. "You sick?"

"Just tired. A lot of things going on."

"Anything I need to know about?"

She laughed. She hadn't meant to, but she laughed, then the laughter turned to sobs. "Oh yes, I'd say you need to know. But not now."

The line went silent. Then, "Have you been drinking?"

"Not yet, but I intend to do so."

"What in God's name is going on? You haven't sounded right the last couple of calls. Lindsay, I'm trying like hell to save my business and I need your support."

"Support. Yes. It is important, isn't it?"

"What's that suppose to mean?"

"Never mind. You wouldn't believe me anyway."

"You're talking about that ghost business, aren't you?"

"I don't want to discuss it right now. I'm too tired and it's too big a subject. We'll talk about it when you get home."

She hung up before he could respond. Ignoring the subsequent rings, she clicked off the volume and headed for the sofa. With thoughts of Galen and the hope he would appear again that night, she quickly fell asleep.

Chapter Thirty

When she woke, evening shadows filled the parlor. Good, maybe it wouldn't be long before Galen returned—that is, if he did. He had to; she couldn't bear another day if he didn't.

Still in her tee and panties, she nuked day old coffee and checked messages on her cell—all from Eric demanding she call him.

Should she? Most likely he'd be at Mark's home by now and could find a private place to talk. She owed him an explanation, but as before, the timing was in question.

She took her cup to the porch and watched the sun set over the far shore. Shrieking sea gulls circled over the water. Several motor boats buzzed by filled with people laughing, talking, or fishing, people with joy in their lives.

How little joy she had felt in her life.

Why was that? Karma? Was she being punished because of her actions—or inaction—as Berina?

She thought of Galen as Berina had known him. How handsome he'd been, how noble. He had wanted to tell Frida about their love, but she, Berina, had stopped him.

Would they all have led happier lives if she and Galen had done the honorable thing and told the family about their love? Surely there would have been heartbreak, but perhaps Frida would have eventually found someone else. And Galen would have lived a normal life span.

What tragic lives they all led because of her decision. No wonder she had felt such sadness when she had first seen the house that evening with Eric.

And she was about to hurt someone else with another of her decisions.

Yet would Eric be that hurt? If he was no longer physically attracted to her, wouldn't he be relived she was ending their marriage?

Should she return his calls? And tell him what was happening? She knew from past mistakes she should be honest. Like Frida, he would be upset at first, but she had no doubt he could make another, happier life for himself with someone who truly loved him. The sooner she ended their marriage, the sooner they could each make a new life.

Eric. Her husband. If it hadn't been for him, she would never have returned to Minnesota. Or this house. How strange the fates are.

She had felt so fortunate when they'd met, and she would never have believed she would be the one to fall out of love. A stab of guilt pierced her, but she owed him her honesty. Never again would she hide her feelings to please someone else.

She picked up her phone to call him and walked to her favorite place in the house, the dining room window through which she could see the tree. To give her courage.

She punched in the numbers. When he answered, she said, "I have a lot to tell you."

**

Sometime later, Lindsay opened a can of soup. The next few days would be long and strenuous and she needed her strength.

Eric had been shocked when she told him everything. Incredulous. Disbelieving. All of it. But she continued in spite of his protests and didn't stop until she had told him everything up to this day.

"I know how this must sound," she'd said. "But it's all true and I felt you should know. When you get your business affairs in order, you need to come home so we can decide what to do." For the first time since she had met him, Eric was nearly speechless, and even when she had finished, he'd said very little.

What were his thoughts now? she wondered. Did he believe her? She doubted it, but that was his concern. She had done what she felt was right.

She took a bite of her soup and chewed with surprise. What was it? She had opened the can without paying attention, but it was delicious. Clam chowder. Her appetite was back. Not only back, but she felt ravenous. Amazing what a clear conscience can do for the soul. She finished the helping and emptied the rest of it into her bowl, then dug in the freezer for some ice cream.

After loading the dishwasher with the odds and ends from the past few days, she turned and looked at the shiny new kitchen. Then she walked into the dining room, admiring her parents' or Berina's parents' dining suite. She hadn't really noticed how nice it all was when she lived as Berina, but now she ran her hands over the glossy mahogany table and sideboard.

She'd have to find a new place to live after the divorce. After all, Eric was the one who had inherited the house and it was legally his. She certainly couldn't make a claim in court. If she did such a foolish thing, she'd wind up in a straight jacket.

Would Galen follow her to a new home? He must. She didn't want to live another life without him.

***

As soon as she entered the bedroom, she knew he was there. It wasn't just the hint of Bay Rum; the very air felt different, even heavier than it had before.

"Galen, you're here. Please let me see you."

She scanned the room, but saw nothing. Was something wrong?

"Galen?" She waited for a sign of him, but there was nothing.

Was something wrong? Should she do something? Go to a different room? It seemed crazy, but she'd do anything just to be able to speak to him again.

The silence stretched on. Just as she thought something had happened and he'd left, the air went very still. Her skin tingled and the hairs stood as if a lightning storm were exploding above the house. Sparks of static electricity appeared and gathered in the far corner of her room, sparking and crackling up and down in a pattern. The air shimmered and waved in a vague outline. A man. Her heart pounded in anticipation and excitement.

Then, in the space of a heartbeat, he stood before her, first as a shadowy form, then, as she watched in awe, the form became solid. Galen.

She wanted to run to him, throw her arms around him, but she felt chained to the bed, unable to move. When his image was complete, he crossed the room to stand before her. Silently, his eyes full of love, he took her hand and drew her to him.

Joyously, she embraced him, wrapping her arms around him. He was there, finally there with her. She stood, her head on his shoulder, her cheek next to his, breathing in the scent of him, content just to hold him.

He wore a shirt and trousers from his era, and he felt the same as he had when she was Berina. His cheek was soft, freshly shaven. She wondered for one insane moment if ghosts shaved. Or bathed, or dressed or did any of the rituals humans performed every day. Maybe she would ask him. Later. Right now she couldn't get enough of feeling him in her arms.

After an eternity, his grip tightened. His breathing quickened, and he ran his hands up and down her back. He nuzzled her face, her cheeks, her neck. When his lips met hers, she returned his kiss with a yearning long denied.

Her knees weakened and gave way. He picked her up and placed her gently on the bed, kissing her until she couldn't breathe, couldn't think. She didn't let go of him, couldn't take her arms from around him. He eased down next to her and they lay side by side, simply holding each other. She ran her hands down his side, his back, then caressed his check, his mouth.

"You feel so real."

"I am real—in your mind, your heart."

"How is it that you're here? Actually here with me in this house?"

"I never left."

"Never?" She wanted to ask him more, but he kissed her again, this time with the passion of a man wanting a woman.

She wanted him desperately, but wasn't ready to consummate their love. The wonder of having him, physically, with her was too great and she wanted to hold him, to look at him, to convince herself he was truly there.

"I've waited so long," he whispered urgently, kissing her again, tasting her mouth, her tongue. "Let me love you." He ran his hands over her shoulders, her breasts. Cupping her buttocks, he pressed her to his hardness. She felt his erection. He was a ghost; how was this possible?

"Oh my darling, I love you so ..." He ran his tongue over her lips, then gently sucked, the sensation sending pleasure waves to her toes. Her nipples hardened. He ran his hands over each breast, then eased her shirt over her head. "You're so beautiful."

She sighed and ran her hands through his hair, pulling his mouth to hers once again in a deep kiss. When they broke, he took a nipple into his mouth. Every nerve in her body caught fire. Her skin tingled. She closed her eyes, the sensations spreading liquid desire through her body.

He caressed her hips, her buttocks, and when he eased his fingers inside her panties and touched her, she nearly forgot to breathe.

"Galen, oh my God ..." she murmured, her passion building to an uncontrollable need, and she no longer cared how anything was possible.

He slid down the bed to roll off her panties. Once they were off, she unbuttoned his shirt, running her fingers over his shoulders, his chest, his nipples. She pushed her breasts against his skin, glorying in the sensation of his flesh against hers. She tried to loosen his trousers but she fumbled in her haste. He took over and in the space of a heartbeat, pulled off his clothes and dropped them by the side of the bed.

They lay melded together, skin against skin, looking into each other's eyes, consumed with the wonder of finally being together. Her need for him built feverously and she kissed him, her passion shocking her. She slid her leg over his thigh, straining to get closer, demanding release.

He moved over her, his eyes locked on hers, and when he entered her, she cried out in pure ecstasy, a fulfillment of two lifetimes.

Chapter Thirty-One

As soon as Lindsay woke the next morning, she reached for Galen, but she was alone in the bed. Confident he'd return soon, she snuggled into her pillow.

Her skin still tingled from last night, and she smiled. Never had she felt anything so intense. She had enjoyed intimacy with Eric and her first husband, but it was never like last night. Galen's lovemaking was everything she had thought it would be, and for the first time in her memory, she felt happy. Deliriously content, fulfilled in every way. To finally be with the one man your heart longed for was an incredible thing.

She yawned and realized how heavy her eyelids felt. If she didn't make herself stay awake, she could easily drift back into sleep. Strange.

She checked her bedside clock. Nearly noon, so she'd had plenty of sleep. When she turned her head, she became aware of a dull throbbing in her temples. A headache. She'd take something for it after breakfast. Or lunch, if she'd be able to eat. The idea of food made her stomach recoil.

When she tried to rise, her body felt heavy, as if she had gained several pounds overnight. Even her arms felt weighted down.

She fell back onto the pillow wondering what was wrong. From a distance, she heard her cell phone ring. Probably Eric. She should talk to him, but she had left her cell in the dining room, and by the time she pulled herself out of bed, the ringing had stopped.

Her legs trembled, and she wondered if they'd hold her. Propping herself against the bed, she pulled on her t-shirt and stepped into her panties.

What was wrong with her? She hadn't felt so weak in years, since that time in the hospital under an oxygen mask with pneumonia.

No pneumonia lately, not even a cold.

From downstairs the house phone rang, but she knew she'd never make it in time. She let it ring until it too, stopped.

She donned her slippers, and slowly, like an old woman using the walls and rails to steady herself, descended the stairs.

She'd call her husband as soon as she felt more steady. Even if something catastrophic happened and she never saw Galen again, she couldn't have a life with Eric. She must make him understand that.

In the kitchen, she made coffee and popped bread into the toaster. Maybe something solid in her stomach would help the fatigue.

Where would she live after the divorce? The house was legally his, and though she never wanted to leave, she couldn't make a claim. Even if Eric believed her, she wouldn't feel right taking his house.

She took her cup to the porch and stood looking over the water. Before her, Serpent Lake shimmered an iridescent sea green under the morning sun. Clouds rolled by, sending wavy white reflections to the undulating water.

If she were dressed, she'd sit on the beach and just drink in the sight. Even from the porch, she could detect the slight fishy smell mixed with damp earth that always seemed to permeate the shore and realized she didn't find it unpleasant. Even the occasional acrid odor of a skunk was better than the layer of exhaust fumes hanging over the southern California freeways.

She supposed she'd find a smaller house next to the lake, although to be near and not live in the Peterson house would be painful—but not as unbearable as living the rest of her life without Galen.

She couldn't think about it today. Already her little burst of energy from the coffee was waning.

Back in the kitchen, she checked her voicemail. She was right. Eric. She didn't have the energy to listen to his rant, so she clicked off the phone.

Something catastrophic… never see Galen again.

What an unconscionable thought. If that happened, she wouldn't want to live—which was the way she'd felt as Berina.

But was that the right way to feel? She poured another cup of coffee. She had been reborn, surely for some purpose other than to mourn his loss again.

Thank God he was with her now.

But, she froze, the full realization hitting her, what if she moved? Would he follow her to the new house, or was he bound to this one?

The thought she might possibly lose him again sent waves of terror though her. Her heart skipped a beat and took her breath. No, that couldn't happen. That couldn't be their fate, not after all that had happened in the past. Not now, not when they found each other again.

She had to see him. Now. He had to assure her they would be together always.

"Galen? Are you here? Please come to me, I need you."

Only silence answered her.

Where did he go when he wasn't with her? What did he do? She ran to the parlor, searching for him, calling his name. Tears flowed down her cheeks. Where was he? Why didn't he hear her?

What little strength she had felt was fading fast and her knees were giving way. She had to lie down. Just for a moment, she thought, sliding down on the sofa, her eyes closing as soon as she hit the cushion . . .

Sometime later, she heard a voice.

"Berina, are you ill?"

Lindsay opened her eyes. Galen stood over her, concern in his eyes. She rushed up and locked her arms around his neck. He was there. Tears of relief formed and trickled down her cheeks.

"My darling, what is wrong?" He took her arms from around him and looked into her eyes. "Why are you crying?"

"I was afraid I'd lost you."

"Lose me? Why would you think that?"

She sighed. The house sat in darkness, rays from the moon streaming through the front windows. She must have slept for hours.

She rubbed her eyes. "What time is it?"

"Late. Aren't you well?"

She reached for him. "Hold me, Galen. I need to feel your arms around me."

He drew her to him, and she held him as if she were trying desperately to hold onto a fantasy that could fade away. He wore similar clothes to the night before, and she caught the subtle scent of Bay Rum. Once again she rested her head on his shoulder, content to feel his warmth, his strength, glorying in the miracle that allowed her to be with him.

"You're trembling, my darling. You should be in bed." He lifted her into his arms, and she lay quietly as he carried her up the stairs to her bed. He could carry her to eternity and she wouldn't care—as long as she was in his arms.

BRENDA HILL

Lying on the bed, she reached for him. "Hold me, make love to me again. I want to feel you inside me."

He sat beside her and took her hand. "As much as I ache for you, I must not. Clearly you're not well and until I know differently, I'm assuming it's because of last night."

"But—"

"I won't risk it, Berina. It took every source of energy I could summon to appear to you, and I'm afraid part of it came from your life force. Until I learn how to overcome that, we must be content to simply be with each other without anything more."

"I can't bear the thought of never holding you again."

"My darling, I must be firm. I refuse to endanger you further."

She was silent. While she loved him even more for his consideration of her, she couldn't bear for him to leave. Not now, not when she desperately needed to be reassured.

"At least lie next to me. Talk to me, tell me about the mysteries of life—and death."

He laughed. "Oh, the mysteries of life. I wish I had it figured out."

His deep, rich laughter sent tingles of delight through Lindsay, and the thought of never hearing it again was more than she could bear.

"Galen, what would happen if I had to leave this house? Would you follow me?"

"Why would you leave?"

"I would have to if Eric and I divorced. This is his house."

"But your father built it. You grew up here."

"That was in a past life, something I could never claim in court. If I said anything like that in pubic, I'd be locked away."

He stared at her, the full understanding dawning on his face. "I don't know, my darling. I've never questioned what might happen. I had only one purpose—to wait for you."

"How did you know I'd return?"

"I just knew. And waited."

"We have to figure this out. We have to know what's likely to happen so I can make plans. I couldn't bear it if I lost you again. I wouldn't want to live."

He gently brushed her hair from her face and stroked her cheek. "No matter what, our love wouldn't end."

"That's a wonderful philosophy, and maybe I'm too selfish, but it's not good enough right now. Help me, Galen."

"Let's get you well. Then we can talk."

"We don't have the time! Eric will be home as soon as he can smooth out his business, maybe sooner. I need to know what to do before he arrives."

"How can I help?"

"Tell me what your life is like now. Maybe we can discover a clue, a sign to guide us."

At his nod, she began. "Do you ever see anyone from the family who's crossed over?"

His face clouded. "No."

"Were you here after … you were shot? When I lived as Berina?"

"I had to see you. Even though I couldn't touch or speak to you, I had to be near you."

"Did Frida know you were there? Is that why she wanted this house burned down?"

"I never wanted to frighten anyone; I simply wanted to be near you. Tilly and Elsie, her young helper, always knew I was there, and I think you did as well."

"I met Elsie," Lindsay said.

Galen nodded. "You always knew when I was near you. Frida also sensed me and was frightened, but she needn't have been. I've never blamed her for that night. It was I who was responsible for everything …" His voice trailed off, followed by a few moments of silence. "After your days ended as Berina and you passed on," he said, "I stayed. I needed to be surrounded by your things."

"I don't remember my last days as Berina. But once she, I passed, why didn't I see you?"

"I don't know why or how things happened, but I suppose it's because I never left this house."

She was shocked. "You never left? Why not, Galen? Didn't you want to go *to the light* as I've heard people with near-death experiences say? According to most, it's a wonderful experience."

He was silent, seemingly considering what she had said. She patiently waited, desperate for some indication as to what had happened. And why.

"I couldn't risk it," he finally told her. "You see, I had betrayed Frida and that was a blight to my character. Who knows what would have awaited me? Besides, somehow I knew you would be back and I had to wait. No matter how many years. Time didn't matter. Only the chance to see you again."

"But that still doesn't tell me how you knew I'd be back."

"When you left, it was different, somehow, so I hoped. And waited."

"What about your own family? Did you have relatives in the area?"

"An older sister in Ironton. Once I got the job at the bank, I moved from the Cities to stay with her family."

"Have you tried to visit them, to see if they're still here? You might have relatives nearby. Isn't that exciting?"

"Possibly ..." His voice weakened and his image was wavering. Lindsay thought it fascinating how he could be solid one moment, then nearly transparent the next.

She realized she too was losing energy. Even though she felt an intense need to know more, she was finding it difficult to think, to form words. She yawned.

"Okay, that's enough for now." Galen leaned over to kiss the tip of her nose. "You need nourishment, but you're in no condition to prepare something. This is one of those times I wish I were more than what I am. But that's not the case, so I want you to call Elsie's granddaugther and ask her to help you. Doesn't she work at a restaurant? Ask her to deliver at least two meals, maybe more. You can put some in the refrigerator for later."

"Shirley. I'll call her." She picked up her cell phone to call, and after she clicked the numbers, she looked up at Galen, but he had disappeared. Vanished.

"Galen?" But there was no answer. By then, someone at the diner answered. Luckily, Shirley was working, and when she came on the line, Lindsay told her she was ill and her husband was still out of town. Could the restaurant make a delivery?

Once arrangements were made, Lindsay felt overcome by exhaustion. She lay back in bed and closed her eyes.

"Thank you, Galen."

His scent filled the room. Comforted, she fell into a deep sleep. She didn't even hear when both phones rang again.

Chapter Thirty-Two

When she woke the next morning, she was alone.

"Galen? Are you here?"

He didn't answer and she didn't sense his presence. He remained in his own world—wherever, whatever—that may be. She just hoped he wouldn't stay away too long. They had to figure out how to remain together, and they had to do it now, before Eric returned.

She sat up and realized she felt stronger. And hungry.

Did Shirley bring the food last night? She slipped out of bed, and, too hungry to bother with her hair or a robe, she took one stair at a time. Clinging to the walls and banister, she made it downstairs, and there on the porch, just outside the front door, sat three white paper bags.

Eagerly, she carried the sacks to the kitchen and unpacked. Six nourishing hard-boiled eggs, four large containers of homemade chicken and wild rice soup, rich and creamy with carrots, celery, and onions. To her delight, she found Hungarian goulash, thick with hamburger, pasta, tomatoes, and cheese. All she had to do was zap it in the microwave. Shirley had sent enough to last a couple of days. Lindsay's eyes welled. What a nice thing to do.

While waiting for the soup to heat, she picked up her phone. When the restaurant answered, she left a message for Shirely, thanking her. She'd settle with her as soon as she felt better.

After hanging up, she rummaged for Katie's phone number to make an appointment, but when she called, a recording stated the team was in the northern part of state doing an extended investigation, that Katie would call when they returned. Disappointed, she made a mental note to find someone else.

Just as she took a bite of the soup, she heard a car pull up outside. She tensed.

It couldn't be Eric, could it? Please, no. Not him. Not yet.

Listening intently, she stood waiting until the front doorbell rang. She released the breath she hadn't even realized she'd been holding. It wouldn't be Eric; he'd simply use his key. Thank God.

Shirley stood at the door. Although casually dressed in jeans and a short-sleeve shirt, her French twist looked as elaborate as before.

Lindsay grabbed and hugged her as if greeting an old friend.

"Thank you for the food," she said. "That sounds so inadequate, but I'm very grateful."

The woman flushed. "Had to check on you. You sounded at death's door last night and I had to make sure you're still standing. Certainly don't want to deal with another ghost at this old place."

"Speaking of ghosts, I need to talk to you about this one. Do you have some time?"

"I have some errands to do for my grandmother, but I'm off today. So yeah, I have time. What's up?"

"I need your help." Lindsay pulled her into the house. In the kitchen, she poured coffee for them both and finished her soup. "Delicious. Thank you again. Before I tell you my problem, how's your grandmother? Is she recovering?"

Shirley shook her head. "They don't think she'll make it."

"I'm so sorry. I wish I could help."

"If it's her time, there's nothing anyone can do. I'm prepared."

Once Lindsay placed her bowl and spoon in the sink, she turned to her new friend.

"I have a lot to tell you. What I have to say will be hard to believe, but just listen with an open mind. When I'm through, I'll answer any questions you might have."

She took a deep breath and told Shirley nearly everything that had happened since arriving at the house, about her experiences with Galen, only skipping the details about their lovemaking. She talked about how she came to believe she had lived before as Berina. Most of all, she spoke of her love for Galen and of his for her, and how fulfilled she felt after finding him again.

Shirley listened with her eyes wide and mouth open at times, but she didn't interrupt. Finally, when Lindsay grew quiet, she spoke. "He actually appeared? You saw him?"

Lindsay nodded.

"What does he look like?"

Lindsay smiled and relaxed. "After all that, you want to know what he looks like?"

Shirley shrugged. "I've heard a lot about him. Two women in love with him …?" She flushed and shrugged again.

"After trying—and failing—to convince my own husband that it's all true, I can't tell you how much your belief means to me. Instead of describing him, go take a look. See for yourself."

Shirley went pale. Her eyes grew wide and she cautiously looked around. "You mean he's here now? I don't think I want to see a ghost …" She glanced nervously in all directions.

Lindsay laughed, something she hadn't done in quite a while. But she wouldn't have believed how much of a relief it was to talk to someone who didn't scoff.

"Relax. He's not here now. At least I don't think so. I meant his portrait. The one I painted right before meeting you in the park that day."

Shirley jumped up. "I'd love to see it. Where?"

"The attic. Go on up. You'll see the stairs on the second-floor landing. I'll wait here."

After Shirley flew up the stairs, Lindsay straightened her tee. She really needed a shower.

Shirley returned and sat in the same chair. For once, the talkative waitress was silent.

"Well?" Linsday said.

"I can see why both women ... uh, you ... and uh, Frida ..." She shook her head. "I don't know what to call you. Lindsay or ...?"

"Lindsay."

"I always believed there was a ghost here, but this is unreal." Shirley asked a couple of questions about the initials, so Lindsay led her to the dining room window and pointed out the ash tree. "You can go look if you want."

"Oh no, I believe you. It's all so bizarre, but I guess I shouldn't feel that way, not after cutting my teeth on grandmother's stories. You said you needed my help?"

"You've lived here all your life, so you must know people. I need a psychic. Or a medium."

"A medium? Seems like you can talk to your ghost without anyone's help."

"You don't understand. When my husband and I divorce, I'll probably have to leave this house, and I don't know if Galen will be able to follow me. *He* doesn't know. I have to find out what to do so we can be together."

"You really want to live the rest of your life with a *ghost?*"

"I can't lose him again," Lindsay whispered fervently. "I just can't. I need someone who has a knowledge of these things, someone who can see into the spiritual realm and can guide me."

Shirely said nothing.

"I know how this sounds," Lindsay said. "That's why I can't ask just anyone, and I don't want to check the Yellow Pages. Do you know anyone?"

Before Shirley could answer, Lindsay's cell rang. It was Eric. Taking a deep breath, she picked up the phone and walked to the dining room window.

"What in God's name is going on there?" he said as soon as she answered. "I've been worried sick. I'm on my way home and should land in Brainerd at nine tonight. Will you pick me up?"

Even though Lindsay had been expecting it, a sense of dread tightened around her as she hung up, suffocating her with doom. This was way too soon; she hadn't had a chance to settle everything—and, she'd only had one night with Galen.

Tears forming, she sought and found the ash tree. Would her time with Galen be cut short again?

"Shirley," she said, walking back into the kitchen, trying to control her urgency, "I need someone *now*. Today. And since I'm not well, I need them to come to the house. I know that's a lot to ask, but can you help me?"

Chapter Thirty-Three

By three that afternoon, Lindsay had taken her shower and was just finishing an egg and toast for strength when the doorbell rang. She didn't know what she'd expected, but not the woman who waited on the porch.

Linda Monson Powell could be any middle-aged woman in her jeans, deep purple tunic, and silver-strapped sandals. No bandanas, no rows of beads around her neck or covering her wrists. She stood nearly as tall as Lindsay, and natural silver strands sparkled through her shoulder-length chestnut hair.

"Thank you for coming so quickly." In spite of Shirley's assurances, Lindsay had felt some apprehension, but was desperate enough to take her chances.

The warmth in the medium's brown eyes put her at ease.

"After Shirley explained the situation," Linda said, "I knew I had to be here. I just hope I can help."

Thank God for Shirley. Lindsay led the way into the parlor. She'd treat the waitress to dinner at a resort on the lake, but that couldn't begin to demonstrate how grateful she felt.

Linda followed her hostess from the foyer, but hesitated just past the parlor's entrance.

"This room holds much sadness," she said. "Shock, agonizing grief. A spirit's departing. More sorrow."

Lindsay stared at the woman, much like Shirley had gaped at her. "Yes," she acknowledged, reluctant to say more. She needed to confirm the woman was authentic. Oh please, she silently begged, let her be the real thing. She needed help that only a true clairvoyant could offer.

"Would you rather be seated in a different room?" Lindsay asked. "We could go across the hall to the family room."

"This will do fine." Linda strode to the parlor chair opposite the sofa. "We'll work *in the middle of the action*, as they say."

"Shirely referred to you as a medium. What's the difference between what you do and a psychic?"

"A psychic reads for the living, such as the client's love life, career, or health issues, but a medium makes a connection with the deceased. Usually in the form of messages from loved ones who have crossed over, or images from spirits."

"You're what I need, then. I don't know how much Shirley told you—"

"I never want to know details," Linda interrupted. "It inhibits my ability to remain open and receptive. I have to admit, though, everyone in the area has heard stories about the restless spirit inhabiting this house."

Lindsay's breath caught. "Will you still be able to be receptive? I so desperately need your help."

"Don't be concerned on that level, dear. I purposely avoided learning details—in case Miss Peterson called upon me. However," she added with a sigh, "that never happened. That's all right, though. My guide will help me learn what I must to help you—if the spirits are willing."

If the spirits are willing? Oh no, Lindsay thought. Another obstacle? "You mean they might not want to help?"

"That's always a possibility, so we must be prepared. Don't be alarmed, though. If Spirit doesn't come through, my guide, Nakhmet, will provide the information I need. As a high priest to the first dynasty pharaoh, his wisdom and knowledge was bequeathed from the ancients before him."

That sounded like something from a 'B' movie, but Lindsay went along. She didn't care where or from whom Linda got the information—as long as she got it.

Linda breathed deeply. "Let's begin."

Fascinated, Lindsay watched as Linda gathered incense sticks from her tote, set them in a holder and lit them, all the while chanting something about surrounding her client and herself with a white light of protection. Satisfied, the medium sat back in her chair and called upon Nakhmet to assist her, then she cocked her head as if listening to someone speak. Then she thanked him.

When she began to speak, Lindsay took a deep breath, preparing herself for a movie version of a heavily-accented guide speaking through the medium; instead, Linda opened her eyes and spoke to Lindsay in a normal conversational tone.

"This house has seen its share of tragedy and sorrow," she said. "But today, it's a happier place. The spirit who resides here is no longer in distress. He's content, although deeply concerned about you." She paused for a moment, then continued. "I see no other spirits stepping forward. If you've been frightened of this entity, be assured he means no harm, and—" she stopped speaking and shut her eyes again before continuing— "he is grateful to be reunited with you. Through him, I'm shown great love such as comes along very rarely. You may live in peace and harmony."

Lindsay waited, but the medium said no more.

"Thank you," Lindsay said, "but that's only part of why I need your help."

Linda studied her client a moment, then nodded. "I know by your aura you're deeply troubled. Tell me. Perhaps I can help."

"You may find what I'm about to tell you hard to believe—"

"'There are more things in heaven and earth, Horatio—'" she quoted, "'—than are dreamt of in your philosophy.' Shakespeare's famous words from *Hamlet*," she said with a smile. "I know them to be true, so don't worry about what I'll believe. Just tell me what I need to know."

Lindsay related the entire story, summarizing when she could, winding up with Galen's concern over her health.

"Incredible," Linda murmured, staring at her client in awe. "I've never met anyone who had experienced such vivid memories of a past life."

"But I don't. I only remember certain things, mainly in dreams, and then only in small amounts."

"It's not necessary for you to remember everything about your incarnation as Berina. Only what is necessary for your life's purpose as Lindsay."

"Life purpose? If you know the reason for all this, please explain it to me. My husband's on his way home because he doesn't believe any of this. He thinks it's ridiculous, that I'm having a breakdown. I have some decisions to make, and without understanding what has happened and why, I'll be making them blindly. I'm terrified."

"Of what, my dear?"

"Too many things could go wrong and I could lose everything that matters to me—mainly a life with Galen, the spirit in this house. Help me understand."

"I'll try to help you, but first I must warn you about your health."

"My health? My health has never been an issue."

"It is now. The spirit in this house is correct. Contact with him drains your life essence. You must cease immediately."

That wasn't what Lindsay had expected. "What?" Her mouth tightened and she stood. "Absolutely not. That's not the advice I need. I need—"

"I've been made aware of the deep love the spirit and you have for each other, and I can't force you to do anything. But please, give me a few moments to explain. Have you heard of auras?"

"Why are you talking about auras?"

"Bear with me a moment longer, please."

Something in her tone struck Lindsay as true. She sat again, still wary, but ready to listen.

"An aura is an electromagnetic field emanating from all living organisms," Linda said, "and they reflect many things about that life form. We humans have them and they can be read by those of us sensitive to them. For decades, the very idea was mocked, viewed with disdain, but today, with our sophisticated technology, they can be photographed."

"Yes, okay. We all have them and they can be photographed. So?"

"I only offer that as proof of their existence, Lindsay. An aura has layers, and they're interrelated, reflecting the person's feelings, moods, and health. Your aura reveals the peril you're in."

"That's ridiculous."

"Is it?" Linda smiled. "How interesting that you used the very word you found offensive when your husband said it to you."

That made Lindsay pause.

"Let me be blunt, Lindsay. You're in grave danger. When I first saw you, I read your aura. The violets are your colors—deep purple, the lavenders, the indigos—all colors of the sensitive. I even see splashes of gold, which suggests enlightenment, guidance for the uppermost good.

"However," she continued, "a different color is growing, swallowing the others. A muddy grayish black, the sign of ill health, of imminent physical danger. If contacts with the spirit continue, you will die. I can't be more blunt than that. If that happens, you will not have followed your own path—and you will not have helped the spirit who resides here."

"I don't understand any of this, and if it takes me away from Galen, I don't want to understand."

"Lindsay, please hear me out. I know your inner spirit will understand. I just need a few more moments of your time."

Lindsay glanced through the windows to outside. It was still light, but the sun was fading. How long had they been talking?

Linda sat back and closed her eyes. The seconds, minutes dragged by and the medium said nothing. Lindsay waited, squirming on the sofa. She glanced out the side window. How long before Eric arrived? During the agonizing wait, she heard the silence—no birds chirping, no seagulls, everything was in stillness as though a cloud of foreboding surrounded the house.

Finally Linda spoke. "Thank you," she said and opened her eyes.

"My dear," she turned to Lindsay, "each of us must follow our universal path in order to enter *Nirvana*, or *Heaven*. It's been revealed that your life purpose in this incarnation is to help this spirit continue on his own path. To do that, he must leave this plane and go through the light. He has been fearful, so you must help him."

"My life purpose is to help Galen leave? No, I won't do that, not when I've finally found him. You can't ask that of me."

"I know of your love for him. That's exactly why you must help him to continue his journey."

"It's too much to ask."

Linda gently took her hand. "Many things are spiraling toward their conclusion, including your husband's life purpose. What you decide now will determine the outcome of several lives—Galen's, yours, and your husband's."

"Eric is involved in this, this plan?"

"His purpose was to bring you here to help you achieve yours. You see, it was destined that you two meet. You both felt an instant attraction that brought you together, but the physical waned, first with him, then with you. His spirit recognized you."

"That sounds as if everything is predestined, as if we have no choice in anything."

"All the fates can do is favorably guide the circumstances, but we, as a people, are endowed with free will. The choices we make, the paths in life we choose, determine our fate."

As much as Lindsay didn't want to lose Galen, Linda's words sounded so true that she felt taken aback. She *had* felt an instant attraction to Eric, something so rare she couldn't explain it, and he *had* brought her to this house.

"Galen didn't want to go through the light," she whispered. "He feels he wronged Frida, you see, and he's afraid to face what comes next. I can't push him into doing what he doesn't want. Who knows? He could be right about what's waiting for him."

"Oh my dear, Infinite Spirit doesn't judge—or punish. All that's waiting for him is what awaits us all--patience, love, and guidance on our soul's journey to perfection. Galen's spirit will find yours again—when it's time. You are destined to be together, so you'll never lose him."

"But if I let him go now, help him cross over, what will I do? I only just found him. It doesn't seem fair to lose him this quickly."

"Ah, but you must. If you continue to see him, to be with him, your body will quickly weaken of its life force and expire. You will have lost him nonetheless, and his journey will stall again."

"But if I died, he and I could be together as spirits."

"Ask yourself why Berina didn't meet Galen's spirit when she passed. It's because her spirit crossed to a different plane, and as Lindsay, yours would do the same. Galen would still be here, condemned to waiting again, hoping you would eventually return. Is that what you want for him? An eternity of waiting? Only you can make that decision."

Chapter Thirty-Four

Lindsay had planned to be at her best when Eric arrived, but when his car pulled in two hours later, she was still sitting in the parlor, so deep in thought she didn't hear his car. She didn't even notice the sun had set and the house was sitting in darkness.

What was she going to do? How could she let Galen go?

Eric's footsteps on the porch alerted her he was home. She jumped up, then faltered. Although she had felt stronger this morning, the day's events had sapped what little reserves she had.

Eric walked through the door, looked around, and flicked on the parlor lights. "Why are you sitting in the dark?"

"Oh, I didn't notice," Lindsay said, her voice weak.

"Are you ill? Is that why you didn't pick me up?"

"I'm sorry," she said. "I forgot."

"You *forgot?*" He set down his suitcase and strode to the sofa, sat beside her, and studied her face. He groaned, then he took her into his arms.

"My God, Lindsay. I knew something was wrong, but this proves you've had some sort of breakdown. We have to get you to a doctor."

She allowed his embrace, but she remained passive in his arms. He still didn't believe her, so that meant she had to go through it all again. She prayed for strength, and the enormity of the entire situation brought tears.

"Don't cry, love. I'm here." He held her again.

He had been a strong influence in her life, and he really was a nice man. She hoped he could put his life back together after this was all over.

"Have you had anything to eat?"

She told him about Shirley's delivery. He stood and took her arm. "I haven't eaten yet, so let's see what's left. We can both have something."

Maybe something more in her stomach would help her get through the next few hours, critical hours that would determine the rest of her life. She let him lead her to the kitchen.

He warmed up the soup and goulash. Knowing how he loved goulash, she took the soup. He chatted about the business while they ate, telling her he needed to get back to California as soon as he felt she was okay, that he thought he and Mark could save the business.

She nodded and made nice noises, all the while wondering how to tell her husband she wanted a divorce.

Once they'd finished their meals, Eric took the dishes to the sink and made coffee. Lindsay wandered to the parlor window and stood looking at the moon's reflections on the lake, entranced by the endless rows of silver strips undulating on the water. Even after all this time, they still looked magical to her. From across the lake, the haunting cry of a loon echoed back to her.

Eric silently joined her.

"It's so beautiful here," she whispered. "I'll hate to leave."

"Why should you leave?"

She turned to him. "Let's sit down. I have a lot to tell you." Once they had seated, she began the story again. She didn't get far until Eric interrupted.

"You told me this ridiculous story—"

"Ridiculous story." She smiled. "Funny. I used that same word with Linda. It's even more poignant now."

"Linda? What are you talking about? Honey, I'll call Mathews in the morning and find out who can help you with these delusions."

"We'll call Mr. Mathews in the morning, but for a different reason. Now I want you to listen to me and don't interrupt until I've finished. If you've ever felt anything for me, you'll do as I ask—for one last time."

"One last time? You're not making sense." He rose and picked up the cordless phone. "Maybe his answering service can get in touch with him tonight." He punched some numbers into the phone.

Lindsay reached over and took the receiver from his hand, threw it against the wall and smashed it. Eric's astonished gaze traveled from the pieces of the phone scattered on the floor back to Lindsay.

"I'm not violent," she said. "Or dangerous, but you must listen to me. All I'm asking is for you to sit down, shut up, and listen. When I'm through, I'll answer any questions you may have." Staring at her, he silently slid down on the sofa.

She began telling him more details about the stories she'd told as a child, stories of life as a young woman in the Peterson house, although she hadn't known the house by that name at the time. She then skimmed through her adult life, only slowing down when she and Eric met. She finished by telling him everything the medium had told her, continuing even though his expression told her he thought she had lost her mind.

When she grew quiet, Eric sat back. "I don't know what to say, except of course I don't believe it."

"What part?" she asked wearily. Even though the telling had exhausted her further, she felt relieved, as if a heavy burden had been lifted.

"None of it. Okay, maybe you told stories when you were a child, but they couldn't have been of this house. I've never heard of anything so absurd."

Lindsay stood. "I was afraid of that."

"You expect me to believe you made love to a *ghost?* And that you were Berina, my aunt?"

"Your adopted aunt, Eric. Your grandparents took me in when my mother—Berina's mother, abandoned her."

"I want to believe you. After all, you're my wife, and I don't want to think you're ... you're—"

"What, Eric? Insane? You might as well say it. That's what you think."

"Lindsay, I spent several summers in this house. If anything was here, I would have noticed it, but I never saw or felt anything. It's just a bunch of superstitious old coots with nothing else to do but spread gossip. Happens all the time. Please, let me call the doctor. He'll prescribe something to help these delusions. That's all they are. Surely you can see that. Perhaps the stress of moving ..."

Lindsay tuned out the rest of his words. He was truly convinced she was insane. How could she convince him of the truth? What could she do? Whatever it was, she had to do it quickly before he had her committed.

She could ask Galen to appear. But what if he were in some other place, the place he goes when he wasn't with her? Eric would hear her calling to a ghost that never appears and be more convinced she was insane. That was too risky. So what else?

Suddenly, she knew what to do.

"Eric, get a shovel and the most powerful flashlights we have. Then follow me."

He stared at her as if she had sprouted two heads.

"Look," she said. "I'll make a deal. If this doesn't work out, I'll go willingly to whatever doctor you choose. But you must follow me now. I promise it won't take long and it's not dangerous."

Reluctantly, he gathered the equipment, even adding work gloves.

"If I'm going to dig, I might as well be prepared. I just hope it's not my own grave."

Chapter Thirty-Five

Lindsay carried a flashlight and led the way to the boathouse, walking confidently on the soft lawn. Eric trailed a few feet behind her. The next few moments would decide her fate: he would either be a total believer and they'd make decisions together, or he would have her committed.

She breathed deeply of the familiar humid air and listened to the night. Insects whined, and from the shore, a soft splash as something, probably a frog, jumped into the water. From above, a multitude of stars twinkled in the velvet sky, a sight so rare in the dense Southern California atmosphere that she still marveled at how close they seemed. And how a part of the universe they made her feel.

How she loved this place, and how she dreaded leaving. She only hoped it would be on her own volition and not strapped in a straightjacket. Everything depended on the next half hour.

"How much farther?" Eric asked irritably, packing a flashlight and two shovels.

"Almost there."

She found the site she wanted near the boathouse, an area of barren grass within the triangle of three pine trees. She wasn't sure of the exact spot as time had erased the guides—the white rocks surrounding a shade garden of wild ginger, purple hepatica, white bloodroot. But she eyed the trunks and stood where she thought they should dig.

"Here." She placed her flashlight on the ground and angled the beam to illuminate the spot.

"Now what?" Eric said, joining her. He dropped the shovels onto the ground.

"We dig." She picked up one of the shovels and cut into the lawn. He watched a few moments, his expression clearly showing his skepticism.

"You promised you'd give me a chance," she reminded him. He muttered something, a curse probably, but he began to dig with her.

After some time, her muscles screaming, sweat running from both their faces, she wondered if she truly were insane. They'd been digging for quite some time and had found nothing. Were they at the right place? She had been sure, but obviously she was wrong.

"Lindsay," Eric said, thrusting the edge of the blade into the ground so the shovel stood upright. He propped an elbow on the handle. "This is madness."

"Please, Eric, don't stop now. It's got to be here. Try a little to your right." She dug almost frantically now. Her future depended on it.

"It's late, I'm exhausted, and—"

Just then her shovel clanked against something metal. Thank God! Eric looked in astonishment at her, then helped dig out the object.

About seven inches long and five wide, the metal chest was so heavily corroded from dirt and weather they couldn't even tell what kind of metal it was. Even without the greenish tint, she knew it was brass.

Lindsay placed it on the ground and wiped it the best she could. An old-fashioned lock secured the latch.

She sat back on the grass. "Do you acknowledge this box has been buried for a long time? Long before you and I moved here?"

"That ground hasn't been disturbed in a lot of years," Eric concurred. "Maybe since my grandparents lived here."

"If I can tell you what's in it, would you then believe my story?"

He shrugged. "That's a lot to ask. Maybe I told you at some point—"

"How could you have told me? You didn't even remember it was here."

He nodded. "Guess you've got me there. Okay, what's in it?"

Before she answered, she paused a moment, scanned the night sky, then faced him. "Do you remember the summer your father passed away," she said, her voice gentle, "and your mother brought you here to stay with Frida and Berina while she worked? You were six."

"Jesus, Lindsay, that was a long time ago."

"Try to remember. It's important."

He shrugged. "I remember some of it."

"You missed your father terribly and was so sad. Berina had lost someone she loved too, so you and she used to talk, to dream about a wonderful future where you'd both be happy again."

"Now you're getting too weird. I could've told you I talked to Berina a lot."

"But did you tell me about the night after everyone was asleep, Berina woke you, and the two of you performed a little ceremony right here by the pine trees?"

Frowning, he said nothing.

Lindsay continued. "I asked you to select a favorite photograph of your father, and I chose one of Galen, and we wrote on the backs of the pictures about how much we loved and missed them, how we hoped one day we would be with them again."

"Lindsay …" he trailed off, his voice ragged.

"We dated them, Eric. And in a little ceromony meant as a symbol to bury grief and sorrow, we put them inside of my favorite jewelry box. And we buried it. You and I, right here when you were six."

He stared at her a few moments, realization dawning on his face.

"My God …"

Lindsay smiled and handed him the box. The lock was so rusted and packed with dirt that he had to use the shovel edge to break it open.

Inside, neatly wrapped in a light blue silk handkerchief, were two faded photographs, both of men from a long ago era. On the backs of each were words of love and loss—one from a woman who had lost the love of her life; the other from a small boy who wept for his father.

Chapter Thiry-Six

At nine the next morning, they were sitting in the attorney's office. Eric had little to say except to answer Mathews' questions about the proceedings.

"Are you sure you want to do this?" Mathews asked again. "Just a short while ago, you two were excited about moving into the house. Now you want to divorce?" He looked from Eric to Lindsay.

"Yes," Eric said shortly. "Let's get it started. And I want her to have the house."

Lindsay still couldn't believe Eric could be so generous. After a sleepless night spent in the kitchen during which Eric said very little, he'd informed her of his decision.

"After all, it's more your house than mine. It should belong to you." All he wanted, he'd said, was to get away, that it was too much for him to handle.

Lindsay understood. After all, it had taken her nearly a lifetime. She wished she could help him, but she knew he'd have to process it all on his own.

Once the papers were signed, they descended the narrow stairway to the sidewalk.

The summer day was glorious. White puffy clouds floated in a azure sky, and the sun brightened the town with a promising day. Residents strolled the busy streets, stopping to greet each other with friendly smiles.

Crosby, Lindsay thought. *Home.*

She still couldn't quite believe Eric had signed everything over to her. No longer would she have to worry about leaving the house—and Galen. She pushed away the thought that he might leave her.

She and Eric stood silently on the sidewalk, undecided as to the next step. Should they return to the house together? That would be awkward, but she couldn't be so cruel as to suggest he stay at a motel. After all, if it hadn't been for him, she would never feel such happiness.

"Want something to eat?" she asked. "It was a long night." For the first time, she felt awkward with him. Maybe because he wouldn't look at her directly or say anything beyond what was necessary.

"Look," he said, his gaze bouncing from one direction to the other. "Let's don't drag this out. I believe you, I believe everything, but I don't need to be in the middle of it. I'll pick up my things and head for the airport. I told Mark I wouldn't be gone long anyway."

"Eric," she began, emotion choking her.

"It's all right, Lindsay." For the first time, he looked into her eyes. And smiled. "It's been an experience, hasn't it? No one could say our life together was boring. But now I need some time to … to put my world together again. I know you'll understand. That's one of the special things about you—you always understand."

***

After Lindsay took Eric to Brainerd's airport for the final time, she pulled into the driveway and just sat for a moment.

Her home, hers and Galen's.

She didn't care how long her life was or how short—as long as she could spend it with him.

As soon as she entered the foyer, she detected Bay Rum. Thank goodness Galen was there. Did he know everything that had happened, that she was free now to love him?

He sat on the sofa waiting for her, and as soon as she entered, he stood. She ran to his open arms and stood blissfully silent, basking in the joy of feeling his arms around her, of the miracle of finally having him with her.

"We're free, my darling," she finally said, holding him close. "Free to love each other without worry."

Finally, he broke the embrace. "Please sit down. I have something to tell you."

Something in his voice caused her heart to skip. Her breath caught. She looked up at him, searching his eyes for the love she knew was there.

She found what she wanted. His love shone through to her, warming her as the sun warms the earth. So what could be so dire?

She sat, bewildered at his expression, at the tone of his words. Was something happening in his world to cause a problem for them? It couldn't be, not now, not when she was free to be with him.

"What is it?" She could barely speak with the dread crushing her, closing her throat, breaking her voice. "What's wrong?"

He sat beside her and took her into his arms. "I was here when the medium spoke, and I listened to her words."

"Galen," Lindsay began, the dread squeezing tighter. She was so attuned to him that she could guess what he was about to say, and she couldn't bear it.

"As much as it hurts," he went on, "I feel she was right. I have to leave."

Lindsay struggled for air. Immediate tears sprang. "No, Galen, you don't," she managed, the panic just below the surface. She couldn't get hysterical now, she had to sound reasonable. "If it's my health, you're concerned about, I don't care. Listen to me. I don't care if my life is cut short again as long as we can be together. We have to have a life together."

"Berina—"

"No! I won't hear of it. I can't lose you now, Galen. I've waited too long." The panic burst free. "Please Galen, don't do this to me. Don't leave me again." She clutched him to her. "I can't bear it." She burst into tears.

He held her and they sat quietly together until the tears stopped. She grew quiet.

"Don't you see?" he said. "If I stay, I'll be killing you just as surely as if I ... shot you. I can't do that. I can't live with the guilt of destroying you."

"Galen—"

"If the medium was right, I'll find you again and we'll have that life with each other. Life, Berina, with you alive and well. Not dying because I'm draining your life source."

"No," she said, but she studied his face and she knew.

"I have decided. Let me go, for your sake and mine."

For your sake and mine. With those words, Lindsay knew it was over. She had to do what he asked. Even though it would tear her apart, she didn't want to comdemn him to stay and suffer more guilt over a perceived wrong.

"All I ask is that you help me." He touched her cheek and gently wiped away a tear. "I can't do it alone."

Her eyes shimmering, she asked, "When?"

"Now, before I weaken."

"Now? That's too soon," she said desperately. "Stay with me today, please Galen. Give me one last time in your arms."

Silently, he picked her up and carried her upstairs in his arms.

An hour later, they lay together, spent from making love. Lindsay's ecstasy was tempered with the heartrending knowledge that he would leave her soon. If only she could delay it, if only—

"It's time," he said, his eyes full of love and sadness. "Help me, Berina."

Even though she couldn't bear his leaving, Lindsay knew she had to do as he asked. She cradled him, much like she'd done when he lay dying from the gunshot. She closed her eyes. What could she do? How could she help him?

"Linda talked about the light," she said, praying for guidance, "and I've heard we all see it. So think about it, Galen. Open your heart and mind. Picture rising above us, above the house, and above the earth. The light will be in front of you, waiting for you, a place of infinite peace and love—"

"I see it! Oh my darling, I don't know how it's happening, but it's coming closer. I'm drawn to it. I want to go." He paused. "It's so bright ... and," his voice dropped to an awed whisper, his face radiant, "it's beautiful. I didn't know it would be like this." He went silent, then in a joyous voice, "My mother ... she's there. She's by the light, waiting, welcoming me."

Fresh tears flowed from her to him. She tenderly wiped his cheek. "Go to her, Galen," she managed, holding him as his image faded.

He reached up to her. "Just one last kiss to take me to eternity."

She tenderly brushed his lips with hers, then he was gone.

Chapter Thirty-Seven

Too numb to cry, Lindsay sat as if in a daze after Galen disappeared. All that remained was the faint scent of Bay Rum, but that was fading as well. Soon there would be nothing left but memories and a fervent hope that Linda was right, that one day they would meet again. She could only trust the medium's words and believe they were destined to be together.

She gazed through the window to blue sky beyond the treetops. Was Galen all right? Would he find the forgiveness and peace he'd longed for? She wished she could have a sign, anything, to know he would be all right.

She closed her eyes. Day turned to night then back to day again. Still she sat. It was as if her body fell into hibernation, waiting.

She dozed.

The doorbell woke her. She tried to ignore it, but it persisted. Irritated, she got up and stumbled to the door.

Squinting at the bright morning sunshine, she scowled at the man standing on the porch. In his late fifties, early sixties with graying sandy-blond hair, he stood a little under six feet. His deep blue polo had a Crosby Police logo above the left pocket.

Police department? What would they want with her? His friendly smile assured her he wasn't about to haul her away.

Suddenly she was aware she hadn't had a shower or even moved from the sofa in … how many days?

"What day is this?" she asked abruptly, wishing she could drop through the floor.

"Why, it's Friday. Are you Mrs. Peterson?"

Friday. Three days after Galen left. "I'm Lindsay Peterson."

"Pardon me, but are you well?" he asked. "Do you need a doctor?"

"What I need a doctor can't provide."

"Ma'am?"

"I'm sorry, I'm being rude. What is it you want?"

"I'm Mike Midthun, evidence tech for the police departent, and Mathews asked me to drop this off on my way to City Hall." He handed her a yellowed business-size envelope.

"Is it a summons about my divorce?"

"Oh no, Mrs. Peterson. It's from the nursing home where your husband's aunt lived."

"Forgive my rudeness. You're right. I haven't been well, but I'm okay." She opened the door. "Please come in."

"Oh that's not necessary. If you're all right, I'll just be on my way." He turned to leave.

"Please," Lindsay said. "I'd like to hear about the nursing home."

"I haven't been in this old place in quite a few years," he said entering the parlor. "I love how you and your husband fixed it up. Looks really nice."

Lindsay nodded. "If you'll pardon me for a few moments …" She didn't wait for a reply before she dashed upstairs to the bathroom for a quick repair.

A few moments later, her teeth brushed, hair combed, and wearing a fresh blouse, she prepared coffee and set the tray on the coffee table.

"Midthun?" Lindsay asked. "That sounds familiar."

"You met my wife, Karen," he said with a smile. "She's the librarian."

"Oh yes, of course. Now. You were trying to tell me about the nursing home."

"Let me explain. Mrs. Simar, the administrator of the nursing home where your husband's aunt lived, dropped the envelope at the police department last night, said an aide found it in the safe. Somehow it was overlooked in Miss Peterson's effects. I took it to Mathews' office this morning, but he asked that I drop it off to you. He said it's Mr. Peterson's property. Will you see that he gets it?"

An hour later, after calling Eric about the letter, during which he told her to open it and send it to him if she felt it necessary, she began reading.

"My God," she whispered after skimming the first two lines. She sat on the nearest chair and reread from the beginning:

Dear Sister, I'm at the end of my life and I don't want to face my maker with what I'm about to reveal on my conscience. I've felt Galen in our home, so if there is life after death, I hope you'll one day read these words.

I'm so sorry for everything I've done to cause you pain. I'm sure I'll have to face the consequences for the sorrow my selfishness has caused.

You see, Galen came to me as the honorable gentleman I knew him to be and confessed he could not continue to see me and certainly could not marry me because he was in love with you. I cried and stormed about, convincing him that it was his duty to marry me. I wanted him desperately, so I lied, you see, and told him I was carrying his child. To my eternal shame, I knew he had fallen in love with you, but during a dance at The Lodge, I carried out an age-old plan to keep him forever. I ordered the drinks and made sure his grew progressively stronger. After he was intoxicated, I led him to his car and kissed him several times.

He passed out very quickly and I drove us home. He slept in his car in our driveway. Papa was extremely upset, and since Galen didn't remember anything of that night, he believed me when I told him we'd gone all the way. That's why he did not break our engagement.

When I shot him, it truly was an accident. I thought someone had broken into our home and was assaulting you. I tried to make up to you the best I could, but of course I could never succeed.

I loved you, and I wish I had been a better person and sister. I wish many things had been different.

Please forgive me.

Chapter Thirty-Eight

That afternoon, after a shower and the rest of the soup from Shirley's care package, Lindsay went for a walk. She had to be outside, close to nature, see the sky.

Walking the rutted road toward City Park, breathing in the familiar scents of pine from the forest, the slightly rotted vegetation from around the lake, and feeling the warmth of the sun on her skin, her heart overflowed with love and wonder. She gazed at the endless sky, in awe of the vast universe beyond.

In spite of her, Berina's, wishes, Galen had been honest with Frida, had been a gentleman after all. Even though Linda had said Infinite Spirit does not judge, Lindsay felt at peace knowing Galen would face eternity with a pure soul.

She cut to the shoreline behind City Hall, moving past the fishing dock and strolled west toward the swimming beach, listening to the sound of water gently lapping the sand. She smiled at the squawking seagulls overhead, and heard the children laughing and shouting from the play area.

Life. How it all seemed so wonderful now. No matter how long of time one was on the earth, that lifetime was beautiful. Miraculous.

She sat on the grass overlooking the water and watched swimmers and boaters enjoying the day. From behind, she heard the clatter of a large diesel pull into the RV parking section. A motor home, she thought without turning to look.

A sharp whistle sounded from the lake, and she watched a man in the water gesture to several teenage swimmers. He pointed to a wooden raft bobbing in the water a few feet beyond the shore. When he blew the whistle again, the teens raced to the raft. The young people had their entire lives ahead of them, Lindsay thought, wondering about their dreams, the goals.

"Excuse me," a male voice said, interrupting her thoughts, the warm velvet tone causing her heart to nearly stop. Galen's voice.

She looked up. He stood in the glare of the sun, and all she could see was a dark outline. But it was enough. Galen.

Her mouth went dry. How was that possible?

She scrambled to her feet and stumbled. When he helped her and she got a good look at him, she could only stare. Except for his darker hair color and, she noticed, his slightly shorter height, he could be an older Galen.

When he smiled, she began to cry.

"Hey, I'm sorry," he said, searching her eyes, concern in his expression. "Anything I can do to help?"

She wiped her tears. "I just lost someone dear. You made me think of him."

"Oh. If you're okay, I won't intrude any longer." He turned to walk back to his RV.

She hesitated only a moment before she ran after him. "What were you going to ask?"

"My name's Gary, and I'll be in town for a few days, following up on some genealogy. My sister discovered we had a great uncle, or maybe it's great-great uncle," he said, smiling, "who lived here years ago. She talked me into checking it out."

Lindsay could barely breathe.

"I'm sick of fast food," he went on, "and I was wondering if you knew of a good place to get a decent meal."

She smiled. "I do."

"You hungry? I know we just met, but can I talk you into joining me?"

Silently thanking the fates, Lindsay slipped her arm through his. "Let's go."

***

At three in the morning, a soft breeze wound through Crosby, lifting above rooftops, whispering through trees, fluttering leaves.

From the north, shimmering waves of the aurora borealis danced across the night sky, undulating in luminous streaks of greens, yellows, and pinks.

The air stilled.

Bubbles formed in Serpent Lake in front of the Peterson home. Ripples appeared and spread across the water. With a soft splash, an elongated head rose, gazed in all directions as if surveying its realm, then apparently satisfied, dipped to disappear below the surface.

Once more, the lake was calm.

Thank you for reading *The House on Serpent Lake.* Recommendations are crucial for writers to succeed, so if you enjoyed this book, please consider leaving a review, even if it's only a line or two. It would make all the difference and would be greatly appreciated.

Thank you!

To see Kahnah'bek's statue in Crosby, visit http://www.cityofcrosby.com/

For updates about my new novels, visit my website or blog,

www.brendahill.com
http://brendahill.wordpress.com/

If you like mystery/suspense, please check my other novels:

UPDATE - Special Edition at a Special Price:

And Justice for Her: Boxed Set of Mystery, Suspense, & Romance Thrillers

From award-winning author Brenda Hill, a boxed set of 3 Mystery, Thriller & Suspense stories of passion, brutality, and justice.

All 3 of her Mystery/Thrillers in ONE set for yourself or give as a gift.

With Full Malice:

Secrets worth killing for ...

A paroled sex-offender shot at close range,
pacts made in hidden chambers ...

Yucaipa, CA, a quiet community in the foothills below Big Bear, hides secrets – extraordinary people, a deadly secret society.

To what lengths will a desperate person go to protect a loved one?

Ten Times Guilty:

A single mother struggles for worth after a vicious attack...a police sergeant seeks redemption for a crime he didn't realize he had committed - until the victim died.

Beyond the Quiet:

After twenty-five years of marriage, Lisa Montgomery thinks her husband's death is the worst that can happen. Then she receives a notice about his secret post office box.

About the Author:

Brenda Hill lives in California and is currently working on her next novel.

She loves things that go bump in the night whether they're serial killers or other strange creatures. She has written about those pesky people who intrude on our lives with deadly force - Ten Times Guilty, With Full Malice, Beyond the Quiet. She's still writing about those pesky people/creatures, but with her latest, a paranormal, they're in a slightly different form. The House on Serpent Lake is a ghost/love story - with a slight twist.

Raised in the South, she lives in the Inland Empire of Southern CA, but longs for cool ocean breezes, the forests and clean air of the northern areas of the States, but can do without mosquitoes and horseflies. The bonus? Her son and his family. So here she stays.

She enjoys hearing from her readers. You can send an email from her website:

http://www.brendahill.com

Made in the USA
Middletown, DE
28 April 2022

64937782R00179